Breaking Free

Pauline Wilson

Boughyards Press

First published by Boughyards Press in 2023

Prologue

The dilapidated wooden bridge over the Yarra River rattled as the cart crossed. As Annie stared blankly, her eyes devoid of emotion, the wrought iron gates at the entrance to a grandiose building came into view. The midday Autumn sun beat down on them, unseasonably hot for this time of year. Huge gum trees lined the river banks, their leaves rustling in the gentle breeze. Although the scent of eucalyptus filled her nostrils, Annie seemed disconnected from her surroundings as she slowly raised her eyes to the tower at the top of the building. The horses' hooves thudded rhythmically on the dirt track until the cart came to an abrupt stop.

"Come on miss, down you get." The sound of the voice jolted through Annie. She found herself seated in a cart drawn by two enormous horses. A hand reached up to help her down. As her feet touched the ground she felt hands grasp both of her arms. She looked to her left and saw that one hand belonged to a tall, angry looking police officer in a full uniform of blue serge trousers and tunic with gold buttons and a high neck. His flat topped peaked cap, complete with the police emblem and chin strap, was pulled down firmly over his eyes. She glanced to her right and saw a similar image.

Suddenly, Annie had a moment of lucidity. Her eyes darted wildly as she tried to take in the surrounding scene. Annie stared at the gate in front of her. Ornate detail was etched into the cast iron structure. She noticed a large spider in the middle of an intricate web within the winding patterns of the gate. Annie felt trapped. She could not understand why she was being manhandled by the two police officers. Her heart beat loudly, her throat tightened and she broke out in a sweat. Her whole body felt like it was being crushed under an immense weight.

"What are you doing? Where are you taking me?" said Annie and she started to struggle against the grip of the two officers.

"Now settle down, miss. You are not well. They will know how to deal with you here."

Annie's dark brown eyes widened as she looked up again at the menacing building with its tall towers at each end.

"Here? What is this place? What have I done?"

But the police officers did not answer because at that moment the gatekeeper emerged from the gatehouse to the right and unlocked the gate. He was a tall man, but bent over by age. His face was crisscrossed with wrinkles, his hair silver grey and thinning. Although his hands trembled as he took the lock from its hook and opened the latch on the gate, his eyes were alert.

He looked at Annie without emotion. "Bring her in." It was obvious he had been through this procedure many times before.

The two police officers moved forward, dragging the helpless Annie between them. She dug her heels into the ground, but it was soon clear that it was useless to try to resist.

Chapter One

Annie sat under a huge gum tree by the creek, not far from the house her family currently occupied in the small mining town of Timor. Spring was finally here which usually would have brightened Annie's spirits. Despite the drought that had gripped the land for many months, there had been some spring rain and daisies and tiny purple wildflowers blossomed in the grass around her.

It was late in the day and as the shadows lengthened, the birds began to sing in the trees. Magpies chortled and a vast flock of cockatoos flew over, squawking loudly as they made their way to their night-time habitats. Annie lay back in the sand and watched the light, swirling clouds passing lazily above.

The sound of a kookaburra laughing overhead brought her out of her reverie. She sat up, kicking the sandy soil with her feet. Her life felt empty. Ever since her father had remarried, they had expected her to look after her younger half-brothers and sisters. She cooked and cleaned and made sure that the children were well behaved. Not that she was not fond of them. She was. Especially her favorite half-sister, Rosa. If not for Rosa and the joy she brought, Annie would have given up long ago. But she wanted more. She was eighteen years of age, and she wanted her own family. She longed to have a husband and a home of her own with her own babies to care for. Her older brothers and sisters had left home long ago. They had been allowed to make their own way in the world. Two of her brothers had married but they had moved to Bendigo, so Annie did not see them and their families often. Her other brother Howard had not yet married but he had his own place back in Avoca. Her older sister Bertha was married to a wonderful man, and they had two babies who Annie adored. But Annie, being the youngest, seemed to have no choice other than to stay to help look after her siblings. She was left on her own to deal with Lillie, her stepmother. It seemed there was no escape. And of course, Cora, her favourite sister, who had been her hope and her strength, was no longer with them. She still missed her sister and confidante desperately.

But was a family what she really wanted? For a long time now she had been troubled by the thoughts that plagued her mind. She did not understand them at all. Was God actually calling her to become a nun? On many a Sunday when she had attended Mass, Father Daly, the parish priest would preach about vocations. The church needed young people to become nuns and priests he had said. As a child Annie had wondered whether she would be one of the special ones who God called to become a nun. She had always prayed fervently and never missed her prayers before bed each night. Once when her mother had tucked her into bed after listening to a lengthy prayer session, she had smilingly suggested that as Annie was so concerned about her prayers, perhaps she should become a nun. Annie missed her mother dreadfully and wondered what she would say now. To this day, whenever Annie prayed thoughts of her mother would come flooding back. Had she really meant it all those years ago that Annie should become a nun? But as time passed and Annie approached her teenage years, she also had dreams of becoming a wife and mother. Why had God put these thoughts in her head? She was becoming obsessed with them. As she prayed each night, she asked him to guide her. And without exception, her mind always seemed to come to the conclusion that her becoming a nun was what God wanted. Could she give up on thoughts of having a family of her own? She felt so confused. Her head would spin with all her thoughts as she wavered between the two options. She longed to be part of a big happy family again. But could she disobey God's calling?

She looked up at the sky. Perhaps it would rain soon. Maybe if rain came, the mine would be flooded and at least they could all go home to Avoca. Her father worked as a mining carpenter at the nearby Grand Duke Mine, which was why they had had to move to Timor. But the sky was stubbornly a bright clear blue, with just tiny wisps of feathery clouds. In any case, she knew it was a forlorn hope because even if it poured, the huge pump, which had been installed at the mine, would deal with any flooding. So no matter how much it rained, the miners could continue working underground to bring up the dirt that would yield the gold. Maybe the mine would be worked out soon. Her father had said that as the time went on, the ground was yielding less and less gold.

She looked at her red, swollen hands and felt sorry for herself. Her stepmother never let her be. Lillie Moore was a tiresome woman. Annie was not fond of her and although she worked hard, Annie never seemed to be able to please the demanding woman. Her emotions boiled to the surface, a fury of heart wrenching pain and desolation. A lump caught in her throat and tears welled up in her eyes.

Annie's toes curled into the sand, and her feet sank into the soft warmth. She didn't think she had the strength to go back to the house and face her stepmother, but knew she had no choice. Her stepmother would be angry. The children would be wanting their tea. She dug her toes deeper into the sand and sighed, knowing she should go but not wanting to leave. She looked out over the creek bed to the paddocks beyond. The heat and the drought had ravaged the landscape. Her relationship with her stepmother was ravaging her soul. But she could not delay any longer so she dragged herself to her feet and trudged back to the house.

Even a year after leaving their comfortable home in Avoca and moving to Timor, Annie was still not accustomed to their new life. There was no catholic church and Annie missed going to mass each Sunday and seeking counsel from Father Daly. The only thing in her life that brought her any joy at all was her younger half-sister, Rosa.

By the time the family had moved to Timor, Rosa had grown into a placid and happy little girl. Now, one year later she had just turned 10 years old. Silky smooth blonde hair framed her face. Annie would curl it for her, winding it in rags to make pretty ringlets. Rosa's big brown eyes were surrounded by the longest lashes Annie had ever seen, and her rosy cheeks glowed when she laughed.

They were sitting outside under the spreading oak tree in the front yard of the tiny timber cottage, watching Rosa's two younger brothers playing marbles, their cheeky faces alive with happiness. The boys drew circles in the dirt and took turns to flick each other's marbles from the ring. They shouted encouragement to each other and laughed heartily when they managed to dislodge each other's marbles from the circle. They were both getting grubby knees and hands from playing in the dirt. Annie was thinking that it was time she got them washed up for dinner when Rosa spoke.

"Why are you sad, Annie?"

Annie looked at Rosa's upturned face and saw the concern written all over it. Annie knew that Rosa was an astute little girl, but still she was somewhat surprised that the young girl had noticed her sombre mood. She decided it would be sensible to be as honest as she could with Rosa.

"I don't really know, Rosa," she replied. "I just feel sad all the time. If only I could do something with my life. But instead, I am stuck here at home."

"Don't you like us?"

"Oh, of course I do. I love you Rosa, and your brothers and your baby sister. But I would like a family of my own one day." Rosa gave a shy little grin.

"Do you have a beau? Who will you marry?"

"No, I don't," said Annie with a sad smile. "That is the problem. How can I find someone when I have to be here working all the time and can never go anywhere to meet anyone?"

"Then you must tell mother that," Rosa said with a self-satisfied smile. She was young enough to believe that every problem could be so simply resolved.

"I have tried, but she needs my help." Annie tried to keep the bitterness from her voice for the sake of the child. She shouldn't be burdening Rosa with her problems. What if Rosa told her mother? Lillie would not be pleased and then there would be more trouble.

Part of Annie's melancholy could be attributed to her relationship with her father. She had long tried to do anything she could to attract his attention and make him love her the way he once had. She desperately wanted to regain the relationship they had when she was a small girl, before her mother had died.

She decided that she needed to try harder to pierce her father's indifference. She knew his grief and his efforts to support his family in hard times weighed heavily on him. Perhaps some small acts of kindness might make a difference. With this in mind, one sunny day in late spring, she walked to the mine to take him a special lunch that she had carefully prepared.

The mine was a hive of activity. The noise of the pump that removed gallons of groundwater from the mine shaft was loud and constant. It had to be kept running to stop the water-logged ground from flooding the mine so that the men were able to work deep underground. It seemed strange to Annie that, although there had been very little rain over the winter months, there was still so much water underground. All around were piles of dirt that had been brought to the surface and then washed in the puddling machine to extract the gold. Men moved among the piles of dirt like so many ants working away at their business.

"Hello miss," said a good-looking young man as Annie paused to look around for her father. She knew she would find him near the huge piles of sawn timber that were used to shore up the mine shafts, which were reaching ever increasing depths.

"Hello," Annie lowered her gaze. She was not accustomed to talking to young men. "I am looking for my father."

"Oh, he is over there," replied the young man. His voice was deep and smooth. Annie had not failed to notice him as she approached the mine. His body was muscular from the hard labour of working in the mine. He had been shovelling dirt into a wheelbarrow, but now he had stopped his work and stood leaning on the shovel.

"How do you know who my father is?" she asked, a slight frown creasing her brow as her curiosity overcame her shyness.

"Sorry miss, I didn't mean to offend. I have seen you here before, talking to your father. You do look very like him you know."

"I see, so you have been spying on me then?" Annie began to feel at ease talking to the easygoing young man.

"Well, I could hardly miss a pretty girl like you," he said with a roguish smile as he removed his wide-brimmed hat and made a sweeping bow to her.

Annie blushed, a little taken aback by such forward behaviour, but she couldn't help but return his smile as she studied him more closely. His clothes were covered in mud and his face was smudged with dirt. Despite this, she could see he was very handsome, with brown hair parted at the side and his dashing moustache neatly trimmed. His dark brown eyes lit up when he smiled.

"My name is Edmund. What's yours?"

"I am Annie," she said with a smile. "I must get on. My father will be waiting for his lunch."

"Wait, perhaps we could meet again sometime?"

"Perhaps." She left him to his thoughts, but as she hurried off towards the pile of timber, she felt his eyes upon her.

Her father seemed pleased to see her and immediately stopped his work. She handed him the picnic basket filled with his favourite lunchtime foods. There were cold mutton sandwiches with pickles, a crunchy apple and a big slab of fruit cake.

"Thank you Annie," he said. "What a lovely surprise."

"Well, mother said that you had forgotten to take your lunch when you left this morning, so I thought I would add something special. I made a cake." She sat the picnic basket down on a pile of timber.

"Will you stay to eat with me? There seems to be plenty for two."

Annie had hoped her father would suggest this. There were very few moments when the two of them could have time to themselves. They sat and chatted as they munched their way through all the food in the basket. Annie felt a glow in her heart as she left the mine. It pleased her that her father had paid her some attention whilst they ate their lunch. But once they had eaten, she knew she must get back to the house. Lillie would be waiting with plenty of chores for her. She said goodbye to her father, packed up the remnants of their lunch, and got to her feet.

As Annie left the mine, she glanced over to where Edmund was working. He shot her a bright smile and a quick wave before he continued on with his work. Annie pondered the feeling of elation that was causing butterflies in her stomach. Could it just be that her father had been pleased to see her, or did it also have something to do with the handsome young man?

Annie took one last look at herself in the mirror. Her eyes sparkled and shone with joy, and her heart fluttered with excitement. The day had finally arrived. She was to go with Edmund to the sports day in Maryborough.

"I must ask my father," she had said when Edmund had proposed the idea one day as she left the mine, having taken her father his lunch again. "I am not sure he will allow me to go."

"Your father is a good man," said Edmund. "Come, let's go and ask him now whilst he is eating his lunch."

"Are you sure? He might be angry with you."

Edmund smiled bravely. "I am game if you are."

As they approached Frederick, he looked at them quizzically. Annie smiled. Her father could hardly have failed to notice that she and Edmund had become friends.

Edmund took a deep breath and swallowed. "Hello sir, I am sorry to interrupt your lunch. But I was wondering if you would consent to allow Annie to accompany me to the Sports Day at Maryborough?"

Frederick tried to hide a smile. "Well young man, since you asked so politely, how can I object?"

Annie was amazed. She had not thought for a moment that her father would allow such a thing. Was she really going to be allowed to go all the way to Maryborough with Edmund? She thought her father would insist that she should not leave her stepmother without help, but it seemed she was going to be able to have a day away from the children. Her heart skipped a beat as she contemplated the outing.

"Who else is going?" asked Frederick. "My daughter must have a chaperone."

"There will be a group of us," said Edmund. "My older sister is coming along with a few of her friends. They are travelling all the way from Heathcote on the train to spend some time with me and to go to the sports. It is some time since I have seen any of my family, so I am looking forward to it very much."

"Very well, but remember you are responsible for my daughter and heaven help you if anything were to happen to her."

Annie could not believe her ears. It would be the first time she had ever been permitted to take part in an outing without her family. Perhaps her father was beginning to understand how unhappy she had been lately.

The day of the sports dawned fine and warm. Annie looked out and saw that the sky was completely cloudless and the most vibrant blue she could imagine. She sang gaily to herself as she dressed in her Sunday best frock with dainty buttoned boots and donned a wide brimmed straw hat trimmed with ribbons and flowers. She felt pretty for once in her life. It was hard to feel pretty when her days were full of the drudgery of housework and looking after small children.

She heard the clatter of the horse and cart pulling up outside the house. The welcome sound of cheerful voices accompanied the rumble of the cart's wheels and the jingling of the harnesses. As she watched from the bedroom window, Edmund handed the reins over to his friend and jumped down from the cart.

Then she heard his knock on the door. Annie ran to answer it, picking up her parasol and basket as she did so.

"Goodbye mother, goodbye father," she called and was out the door before they had a chance to call their goodbyes.

Edmund helped her up into the cart, where she greeted the others with a smile. Edmund introduced her to his sister and her friends and soon Annie discovered that his older sister was just as pleasant and friendly as her brother.

"Isn't it exciting? I can't wait to see the grounds and all the events," said Annie.

"Settle down, girl," said Edmund with a smile. But he could not hide his delight at her excitement.

He slapped the reins against the horse's back. "Giddy up." Annie held onto her hat as the cart moved off at a brisk pace.

It was six miles to the sports grounds in Maryborough, so it took a good thirty minutes to get there. But it was all part of the fun. Everyone was talking and laughing happily as the miles flew by. Soon enough they arrived at the sports ground. There was a large crowd in attendance and all were dressed in brightly coloured attire to suit the festive occasion. The well-dressed ladies carried dainty parasols to keep the sun from their delicate skin and a faint scent of perfume wafted in the air. Everywhere there were happy groups who had all found spots under the sprawling branches of trees to escape the full heat of the sun. Edmund, Annie, and the others soon also found their own shady spot. They threw rugs on the ground and unpacked the wicker picnic baskets that the ladies had brought with them.

An appetising aroma emanated from the baskets, which were packed full of such delights as pork pies, cold beef sandwiches, devilled eggs, crunchy apples and bottles of homemade ginger beer to wash it all down.

The sports ground was gaily decorated with flags and bunting, which fluttered in the gentle breeze. There was a brass band playing in the rotunda and refreshments were being served. Local produce was available for purchase at the stalls. The cycling races got underway first and then the foot races. There were some very close races, adding to the excitement of the day. But honestly, Annie was so pleased just to be away from home and spending time with Edmund that she would not have cared if there had been no entertainment at all.

As the festivities continued, Annie and Edmund moved away from the others and walked towards the rear of the crowd, savouring the time they could spend together. As they walked, Edmund slipped his hand into hers and she felt a tingle run through her body.

"Oh Edmund, thank you so much for asking my father to allow me to come with you. It has been the best day I could ever have imagined."

"You deserve it, Annie," he said. "I must say, it is good to see you smiling. But we must rejoin the others now. They will be wondering what has become of us." As they returned to their group of friends, Annie reluctantly released her hand from Edmund's. She felt his gaze upon her but did not return it and wondered if she had offended him.

After a thoroughly enjoyable day, they all loaded themselves back into the cart for the trip home. Annie sat close beside Edmund, feeling the warmth of his leg gently touching hers. She felt euphoric and did not want the journey to end.

But that night, as she knelt to say her prayers, she wondered at the delicious sensation she had felt when their hands touched. Surely that must be a sin? She must control her emotions.

Chapter Two

Annie and Edmund had become firm friends in the weeks that followed their first meeting at the mine. Annie would often make the excuse of going to the mine to take her father's lunch to him. Frederick would smile and gratefully accept the extra attention from his daughter, but Annie suspected he knew very well that the real reason she frequented the mine was to see Edmund.

As their friendship grew, they conspired to have time alone away from the prying eyes at the mine. As often as Annie could slip away from the house and the never-ending tasks of helping her stepmother with the children, she would meet Edmund at their special spot by the creek. Annie had stumbled across this private place on one of her walks not long after she and her family had arrived in Timor. It had become a place of solace for her, an escape from her tedious life. The path beside the creek was surrounded on all sides by tall gums and undergrowth but at this point it opened up onto a shady clearing covered with thick grass which was beautifully green and lush for much of the year, except in the very hot summer months. In the spring it was covered in yellow everlasting daisies and tiny blue pincushions. If you looked closely, the flowers of the pincushions were made up of a lot of smaller flowers. The little space provided dappled sunlight, so on these hot summer days there was plenty of shade. She was pleased to be able to share this refuge with Edmund.

Annie and Edmund spent their time discussing the goings-on in the world. Times were becoming increasingly difficult with the depression worsening. After the boom of the 1880s property prices had begun to fall in 1889 and now in 1893 the Commercial Bank of Australia, the largest bank in the country, had ceased operation. In the newspapers, they read about the struggles of the many people who were out of work.

Despite the dire circumstances, Edmund was fortunate that he had his job at the mine, but they both wondered how long the gold could last and they often worried about the future.

Although Edmund was a mine worker, he was educated, and he shared Annie's love of books. They enjoyed engaging in deep conversations about the characters they encountered in the books they shared with each other.

On this hot summer's day, Annie had brought a rug for them to sit on as the grass was dry and yellow. Edmund spread the rug, and they sat talking softly. A gentle breeze blew off the stagnant ponds of water that remained in the creek. Flies buzzed around them and as Annie watched, a tiny lizard poked its head out from under a rock but quickly retreated as she moved to try to look more closely at it.

Annie had packed a picnic lunch. She had told Lillie that she was visiting a sick friend and would have lunch with her. She needed an excuse to get out of the house, but was also not willing to share the information that she was meeting with Edmund. Lillie would be horrified to think that she was spending time alone with a young man. Annie didn't need that argument today.

They sat munching the sandwiches and cake and then lay back, side by side on the rug, feeling lazy and drowsy now that they had satisfied their hunger.

Christmas was only a few days away. Although Annie wished she could see Edmund on Christmas Day she knew that would not be possible so she had brought a small gift for him today. She had managed to purchase a crisp linen handkerchief at the General Store and had carefully embroidered his initials in the corner.

As she handed it to him she felt a little sad that it could not be something more substantial. But as he untied the string and removed the brown paper wrapping, she could tell that he was pleased.

"Annie, thank you, it is very special. I shall treasure it." He held it up to his nose as he detected the waft of the scent that she had sprinkled on it. "It will always remind me of you. I hope the scent does not fade too quickly."

Annie smiled and breathed deeply. She could smell the cool, salty maleness of Edmund's body as he lay close beside her. He sat up and leaned on one elbow and reached over to touch

Annie, running his rough, calloused fingers over her smooth, delicate hand. She felt a jolt of electricity from his touch run up her arm like a bolt of lightning.

"Annie, I am becoming very fond of you," he said, looking at her from under hooded eyelids, too afraid to look directly at her in case she rebuffed him.

Annie felt her face redden and her body tingle at the feel of Edmund's breath so close. But she was torn. She didn't know what she wanted anymore. Increasingly, she was having thoughts about what God wanted for her. Despite being separated from her religion by their move to Timor, her prayer sessions had not diminished and neither had the conviction that she was being called by God to become a nun.

"Oh, Edmund, I am very fond of you too. But I must tell you that my faith is very important to me. I am convinced that God wants me to become a nun."

"But Annie, you don't even go to church."

"I know, but that is only because there is no catholic church here in Timor. I long to return to our home in Avoca so that I can attend Sunday mass again."

Annie could tell that he was going to say more, and she became nervous. This was not the first time religion had been discussed. Edmund was a catholic too, so he understood the notion of Annie having a calling, of her believing that she was being called by God to become a nun.

"But Annie, I think perhaps what I am feeling is more than fondness."

Annie carefully withdrew her hand, not wanting to upset him because she did indeed have feelings for him. But she couldn't give in to those feelings. She mustn't.

"Edmund, we must not talk this way."

"I understand how you feel Annie, but doesn't God need some of his followers to marry and have children? Are you sure you should become a nun? We have a great deal of affection for each other. Perhaps God is calling you in a different direction."

"Please Edmund, can't we talk about something else? I am so confused. We had better get back anyway. We have been so long. Mother will be angry."

"Where have you been?" shouted Lillie as Annie entered the small, crowded kitchen after returning from her meeting with Edmund.

The children were milling around, squabbling loudly with each other. Lillie sat feeding the baby. She was red faced and Annie could see that she was not coping with the chaos around her.

Lillie never seemed to smile lately. Her stern face showed her age. Her dark hair, greying at the temples, was pulled back in a tight bun at the back of her head. Lillie was 30 when she and Frederick married and now here she was at 40 years of age with a newborn. Annie decided if she was going to marry, she needed to do it soon. If she was going to have children, she wanted to have them when she was young. But even as that thought entered her head, she felt the guilt in the pit of her stomach. God was all seeing. He would know that she had these thoughts.

Lillie glared at Annie with blazing eyes. The two small boys were squabbling over a toy train whilst Rosa tried to referee the fight, which only added to the commotion.

The house really wasn't big enough for the large family of seven. But they had to make do whilst their father was working here. There were two small bedrooms, a kitchen and a wash-room. Annie had to sleep with the children, sharing a bed with Rosa. The two boys slept top to tail in the other bed in the small room whilst the newborn baby girl had a tiny crib in their parents' bedroom. The kitchen was quite large, with a table and enough chairs for everyone to sit together to share a meal. As this was only supposed to be a temporary residence, they had taken little trouble with making the room homier. Not a single picture hung on the walls, not even any decorations. A sturdy, old cast iron stove stood in one corner where all the meals were cooked and the water heated. The stove had to be going all the time, which turned the room into an inferno in the heat of the summer. All the windows and the door were wide open to let in any breeze that wafted in. Hessian bags hanging over the windows did little to discourage the flies.

The only time Annie had any privacy or time to herself was when she slipped away to the creek for a brief reprieve. She was happier now that she had met Edmund and was able to spend some time with him. But she was still dissatisfied with her life and longed to be anywhere but in this hot, crowded house.

"Sorry, mother," muttered Annie. "I just went to see if there was any water in the creek after the rain."

"Well, of course there is no water in the creek. It will take a lot more rain than that to get the creek flowing again. And the water level in the tank is so low we will need to be extremely careful how we use it. If we don't get good rains soon, who knows how we will cope. Now stop dawdling and get on with preparing the vegetables. Lord knows the children will be starving and completely wild by the time we all sit down to eat, thanks to your thoughtlessness. I have no idea what time your father will be home. He seems to be later every evening."

Annie couldn't help thinking that her father dawdled on his way home in order to spend as little time as possible in this chaotic kitchen. She was silent as she went about preparing the evening meal.

"Not like that," said Lillie. "What are you doing? You are cutting the vegetables too small."

Annie looked at her blankly and continued on. She knew from experience there was no use arguing with Lillie. But she felt her face redden as her anger rose.

"Come on, hurry up girl," said Lillie. "The children are hungry." And indeed, the children were becoming rowdier with each moment that passed.

As Annie peeled and chopped the vegetables, the level of noise seemed to rise and her anxiety rose until suddenly she could stand it no longer.

"Be quiet!" she screamed at the top of her lungs. Momentarily the room fell silent. But Lillie's anger soon matched Annie's.

"Get control of yourself Annie. How dare you scream at me and the children?"

"How dare I? I am sick to death of being forced to look after your children. Why should I have to do all the work whilst you sit around with your needlepoint?"

"Needlepoint? I rarely have time for such luxuries, as you well know. You know I have not been well Annie. And I have the baby to take care of. Please calm down. You are upsetting the children." Annie looked around her and indeed the children did seem alarmed, cowering behind their mother. But it made no difference. For some reason she could not calm her mind. It was racing so fast that she felt giddy. She seemed to have lost all control. Her rage was all-consuming, and it felt good to finally let it come to the surface.

"I will not calm down. You have turned my father against me. He doesn't love me anymore. He only has time for you and your children and has completely forgotten about my poor mother."

"You know that is not true, Annie. Your father loves you very much." Lillie seemed alarmed at this outburst from Annie and now tried to calm her. "You just don't see it. He is really pleased that you have developed a friendship with Edmund. He let you go to the Sports Day, didn't he? I know it has been hard for you, but you really must calm down." Annie could see that Lillie was becoming worried now, but somehow that fuelled her anger.

By now Annie was in such a rage that she could not think straight and was never going to see reason. Just at that moment, her father arrived home. He glanced from Annie to his wife.

"What is all the shouting about? I heard you from the road," he said. "What is going on here?"

"Oh father, I hate it here. When are we going home?" Annie was distraught that her father had seen her like this. Now he would hate her even more.

"Annie, calm down. You are behaving like a child. You are a grown woman. What are you thinking, behaving like this in front of the children? This is our home for the time being. I have to be where the work is."

Annie could not be consoled.

"I am not putting up with this anymore. I will leave."

"Don't be foolish Annie, of course you can't leave," said her father. "Where will you go? You must get control of yourself. Now apologise to your mother."

Annie stared at her father, aghast at the suggestion that she could just say sorry and all would be forgiven.

"Apologise? What for? I have done nothing but be a slave to her since she came into our home. I am sick of it father. It is not fair." Annie continued to vent. Her head felt as if it might explode. She could not think straight.

Annie stormed out of the room and threw herself on her bed and sobbed loudly into her pillow. Her father was right. She had nowhere to go. She was trapped right here and had no option but to stay.

Chapter Three

Annie had not had an opportunity to see Edmund for several weeks after Christmas. It had been a busy time with visits from all of Annie's older siblings.

The drought was stretching on. The scorching sun had blazed down on the tin roof for days on end without any respite, making it unbearably hot. The only escape from the blistering heat was down by the creek, where the towering trees offered some shade and there was a chance that a cool breeze might be coming off what little water was left in the creek.

The Bet Bet creek, almost dry after the long hot summer, was lined with cracks that formed an uneven square patchwork on the creek bed. The stagnant pools of water that remained gave off a faint odour of rotten eggs. The surrounding grass was yellowed and dry. The dry baked earth stretched as far as the eye could see. Even the leaves of the gum trees that lined the banks of the creek appeared to have lost their evergreen colour and were now dull and grey.

Annie was feeling at her very lowest when she and Edmund met by the creek and wandered slowly down the winding path towards the clearing.

As they walked, Edmund glanced sideways at Annie. "What's wrong Annie?"

"Oh Edmund, I hate my life. I had the biggest argument with mother after the last time I saw you. She is so mean. Father came home in the middle of it and I felt so ashamed. But I couldn't do anything about it. I couldn't seem to get control of my emotions. Father was so angry with me."

"I am sorry Annie, that is awful. But you must know that your father and stepmother love you. They want you to be happy." Edmund knew how important her father's approval was to Annie.

"How can I be happy in that place? I have been thinking Edmund. Will you take me to Avoca? It is so long since I went to mass. Maybe if I go to confession, God will forgive my sins and I will feel better about everything."

"Of course I will Annie, you know I will. But you must get permission from your father."

Having gained a reluctant permission, Annie and Edmund planned to attend Mass the following Sunday. Annie donned her Sunday best, put on her bonnet and picked up her precious prayer book and waited impatiently for Edmund to arrive.

She climbed up into his cart, and Edmund flicked the reins to get the horses moving. It was only a short trip to Avoca, so they were there in plenty of time for Annie to attend confession before Mass.

In the dark confessional, Annie's hands shook as she waited for the small opening between her and Father Daly to slide back. She could just see his dark outline. In a low fretful voice, she began her confession. They were the same sins she had always confessed as a young girl. She wondered how she could be so wicked as to keep repeating the same sins over and over. But then she mentioned Edmund and her confusion about how she felt about him and whether she was actually being called to become a nun.

Father Daly at once launched angrily into a speech about the evils of fraternising with a man before she was wed. Annie cringed. Her anxiety intensified, beads of sweat broke out on her forehead.

"What am I to do?"

"To begin with you must repent your sins, say your penance, and then you must pray and let God guide you. You will know what to do. He will give you a sign."

Annie and Edmund then attended Mass. Annie let the familiar words wash over her. She prayed for forgiveness.

On the trip home, Annie was withdrawn and Edmund tried to talk to her several times before he was eventually able to get a reply from her. She told him that she was more confused than ever.

"I don't know what to do Edmund. My mind is spinning in circles and I just can't think clearly."

"Annie, you know I care for you a great deal, but I don't know how I can help you."

Annie looked at him angrily. "There is nothing you can do to help Edmund, except bring me to Mass each Sunday so I can go to confession and confide in Father Daly, perhaps that will help me clear my mind."

Edmund looked skeptical and saddened but agreed to take her. Somehow through the fog in her mind she knew that she had hurt him with her angry words but she did not know how to fix it.

Annie knew she must make up her mind. She did not want to be a sinner.

Annie's feelings for Edmund continued to grow. Although she knew she should end her relationship with him, she could not bring herself to do so. He was the only light spot in her life. She knew he was becoming impatient with her indecision. Every time he reached for her hand, she would pull away from him. She had decided she must become a nun and there was no way out of it. Father Daly was quite clear that she needed to stop seeing Edmund if she wanted to devote her life to God.

Since Father Daly had told her that God would give her a sign, she saw signs everywhere. Every time she knelt to pray, it was the first thing that entered her head. She saw no alternative.

The weekend was drawing near and Edmund had asked her to join him at the dance that was to be held at the local hall on that Saturday night. She was worried because she had made her decision. But how could she tell him? She hated the thought that they could not be friends any longer once she entered the convent. Arrangements were not yet finalised, but she had asked Father Daly what needed to be done.

Edmund arrived early to collect her for the dance. She was wearing her usual Sunday dress. After all, there was little point in acquiring any new clothes when she would be wearing the habit of a novitiate before too much longer. Even so, as she curled her hair and arranged it with some pretty ribbons and flowers, and put a touch of powder and lipstick on, she felt she looked quite respectable.

Edmund looked very dashing in his striped suit, waistcoat and bow tie. His hair was carefully combed and shone with brilliantine. It was obvious to Annie that he had put a special effort into looking his best. She could not help but think that he seemed nervous, but perhaps that was just her own nerves as she contemplated telling him of her decision.

"You look as pretty as a picture, Annie," said Edmund as he offered her his elbow and she slipped her arm into his. "I think we might have a storm before the night is out."

"Well, I must say you look very handsome tonight too, Edmund," replied Annie. "I have brought my umbrella in case we are caught in the storm."

They walked the short distance to the hall and as they got closer, they could hear the music being played by the local band. There was a big sign hanging over the doorway. Dance, Saturday 4th March 1894.

There was already a large crowd, and the dancing had begun. The hall was beautifully decorated with colourful bunting strung in rows hanging from the ceiling. There were large vases of flowers on the stage where the band, from Maryborough, was playing. Gas lights burned in the wall sconces. It was a magical scene, like something out of a fairytale, and for a few moments Annie forgot all about the news she would need to break to Edmund.

The room was crowded with well-dressed people, young and old. Annie accepted the invitation to dance with several of the other young men, but the majority of the dances were with Edmund. Around ten o'clock, a delicious supper was served. The older women of the community had slaved for days, making sandwiches and baked treats for the lavish supper.

As the evening drew to a close, Annie became more anxious. She would have to break her news to Edmund soon. The last dance was a slow waltz, and Edmund held her close. Annie savoured this moment as it could be the last special moment that she shared with Edmund. And then, suddenly, it was over.

The rain was just beginning as they made their way home. Annie opened her umbrella as they hurried towards the house. There was a loud clap of thunder and lightning streaked the sky. They ran for it and made it to the verandah just as the rain started pelting down. They sat down together on the swing seat.

Annie and Edmund sat staring at the sound and light show provided by the storm. It was majestic, and the power of nature was something to behold. But there was also turmoil in Annie's heart. She must tell Edmund of her decision. But before she could say anything, Edmund turned to her.

"Annie, I have something to ask you." Annie thought she knew what was coming. She had to speak up now. But somehow the words would not come, and she just stared blankly at Edmund.

"Annie, you know that I have become very fond of you." He paused for a moment and looked at Annie nervously.

"Annie, will you do me the honour of becoming my wife?" At that moment, he pulled a ring from his waistcoat pocket and got down on one knee.

Annie stared at Edmund, her head spinning. She felt faint. How she longed to say yes. But she knew she couldn't. She smiled sadly and grabbed Edmund's hands, pulling him back to his feet.

"Edmund, I am so sorry, but I can't marry you."

Edmund's face crumpled. Annie could see that he was devastated, and it broke her heart.

"Why Annie? You know I love you." Edmund was trying desperately to compose himself and Annie felt guilty for causing him so much pain.

"I do know that, Edmund, but you know what has been on my mind for such a long time. My mind is made up. I am going to become a nun. So I have asked Father Daly to begin making the arrangements."

"No, Annie, please. You must reconsider. Have you told your parents? What do they think of your plans?"

"You know they are not Catholics, Edmund. So how could they possibly understand? You know father does not approve of my dedication to the church. In fact, he approves of very little that I do."

"Annie, I don't understand why you doubt your father so gravely. I am convinced he loves you dearly and is indeed very proud of you. I have not asked you to marry me without first talking to your father. You misunderstand him Annie."

"What do you mean?"

"When I asked him for your hand in marriage, he expressed his delight. He actually told me he knew you were unhappy, and he felt at a loss to do anything about it. I believe he wants nothing more than for you to be happy."

Tears welled in Annie's eyes as she looked at Edmund's kind, handsome face. He really did care for her. But it was one thing for her father to say these things to Edmund. Why couldn't he show his love for her? It just made her all the sadder. And she knew that even if what Edmund said was true, her father would definitely be disappointed with her choice to enter the convent. Edmund was looking at her sadly.

"Is there nothing I can do to change your mind?"

"I really don't think there is. In fact, I feel like the decision has been made for me. I don't seem to have control over my own mind."

"Is that not all the more reason to reconsider?"

"Father Daly says that it is not at all unusual to be confused, but that I must follow God's path."

As Edmund walked away, Annie felt a wave of sadness wash over her. She knew that their relationship would never be the same again, and the thought of hurting him was almost too much to bear. But there was little she could do. She had to follow the path she had set for herself, no matter how hard it was.

Chapter Four

In the days that followed Edmund's proposal, Annie found it harder and harder to focus on her decision. Each night she knelt to pray and hours would pass before she rose. She could not sleep as thoughts of Father Daly's insistence that she must follow her calling looped constantly in her mind. But how could she have turned Edmund down? She realised she loved him too. She was so confused as her mind swayed between telling Edmund she had made a mistake and knowing that she must follow her calling. Her mood swung between anger and numbness and her family bore the brunt of it. One moment she would be berating the children and the next, she would be ignoring them.

Annie's mind was in turmoil. She knew she wasn't thinking clearly. She had to get away from here, from her family, from Edmund. They were all so disappointed in her. Edmund had barely spoken to her the last time she had seen him at the mine. She could not blame him. Her refusal to marry him must have hurt him deeply.

She had eventually had the courage to broach the subject of becoming a nun with her father.

"Father, I need to speak with you. Can you please come outside so that we can have some privacy?"

Her father looked at her questioningly, but he rose from the table where he was reading the newspaper and followed her outside. They sat together on the verandah seat.

"What is it, Annie?" asked Frederick. Annie had butterflies in her stomach as she carefully considered what she would say. How could she find the words to tell her father of her decision? After a few moments of silence, she blurted it out.

"I have decided to become a nun."

"I beg your pardon. What do you mean? Surely you can't be serious?"

Annie sat staring blankly at the ground. She did not know how to explain her feelings to her father. The losses he had suffered had sorely tested his faith.

"But Edmund has proposed, has he not?"

"Yes, he has, but I turned down his offer."

Her father was becoming angry now. "How could you turn down the offer of marriage from a fine young man like Edmund?" Annie cringed and felt the now familiar tightness in her chest. The last thing she wanted was to make her father angry. But she had no choice. She had to go through with her plans now. She was convinced there could be no turning back. Her voice choked as she continued.

"I am so very sad not to be able to marry him because I have feelings for him, but I don't feel that I have a choice. Father Daly has made it very clear that now that the process has begun, there is no turning back."

"You must reconsider, Annie. This is a terrible decision." Frederick stood and glared at Annie for a moment before stalking back into the house.

Now, at the end of another long day, she sat on her bed trying to quieten the turmoil in her mind. It seemed to her the only alternative was to run away from all her problems. She was regretting her decision. Leaving Edmund behind to live as a nun for the rest of her life no longer seemed possible. But if she stayed, she would have to tell Father Daly that she couldn't go through with it and he would be furious, especially as he had started making arrangements. Annie could not put up with her inability to decide any longer. Her stomach clenched as she began to gather her things. As she threw her belongings haphazardly onto her bed, she felt rather than saw the door open and her half-sister Rosa entered quietly. Rosa sat on the bed not saying anything, staring at Annie with wide eyes.

"What are you looking at?" stormed Annie, unable to control her anxiety, despite her affection for Rosa.

"Annie, what are you doing? You aren't leaving?"

"You are the only person who wants me here, Rosa." Annie suddenly felt a strange sense of calm come over her. It was as if she was detached from her surroundings and observing herself from outside her body. "Your mother and my father are sick of me. They have no time for me. The only thing I am good for is being their slave. I need a better life."

"You can't leave. I would miss you too much. Where will you go?" replied Rosa.

"Edmund will help me. He will look after me. He proposed marriage to me after all."

"He did? Then why are you leaving?"

"I cannot marry him."

"But why not?"

"Just because I can't Rosa," said Annie, her voice rising hysterically.

"But how can he help?" said Rosa.

Annie could see the hurt in her sister's eyes, but she just looked at her blankly and continued to pack her belongings into the brown leather bag. She gathered up her few pounds in savings, which she kept in a small box in the drawer of her side table. Finally, she stowed her precious prayer book and rosary beads carefully in a side pocket and closed the catches on the bag. She picked it up and carried it back through to the kitchen.

"Where are you going, Annie?" asked her father.

"I am sorry, father, I can't stay here any longer. I need to get away."

"Don't be foolish. It is late. You can't go anywhere at this hour."

Tears welled in her eyes and slid down her cheeks. In fact, she didn't want to leave her father, but she felt she had no alternative. She had to get out of this house or she would go mad. Perhaps she was already mad. She just felt sad and numb. Her thoughts were confused.

She left the house, slamming the door behind her. Her father followed her into the yard.

"Leave me father, I cannot stay any longer."

"But where will you go?"

Annie ignored him.

Annie walked down the dusty track towards the centre of the small mining town. The shadows were lengthening. It would soon be dark. Her head ached. She was confused, but she felt strangely calm. As the sun sank towards the horizon, the sky turned red like the coals of dying embers in a campfire. All Annie knew was that she must go to Edmund. She walked past the General Store, which was closed for the night, and past the few other buildings in the main street then turned into a small side street. Edmund would help her. She walked on with dragging feet through the fading light until she reached his small miner's cottage.

"Edmund," she called. "Are you here? I need your help." The sound of her own voice, tremulous and uncertain, surprised Annie.

Edmund appeared at the door. He looked at Annie with concern.

"What are you doing here, Annie? You have a bag. What is going on?"

"I can't stay there anymore Edmund."

"Annie, I know you have been unhappy, but where will you go?"

"I hoped you might help me."

"What do you mean? How can I help you? You know I love you Annie, but you have said you won't marry me. Sadly, I have nothing else to offer you. Let me walk you home."

"No!" Annie was becoming hysterical again. Her eyes flashed angrily and her voice rose to a shriek as she fought to control her emotions. "You know I can't go back."

"Annie, please be sensible. Let me take you home." Edmund reached out and grabbed her elbow.

"Let me go. If you will not help me I will make my own way."

Annie pulled away from Edmund's grasp and began to walk back the way she had come. Edmund followed, having to jog to keep up with her as she hurried away.

"Annie wait. You can't do this. Where are you planning to go?"

Annie had not thought that far ahead. If Edmund wasn't going to help her, where would she go? Her head whirled, but she kept walking at a furious pace. She looked over her shoulder to see that Edmund had stopped following and was looking at her sadly. *If only I could marry him*, she thought. She squeezed her eyes shut to try to block out all the conflicting thoughts that were flying around in her head. But they just got louder. She tried to calm her breathing but the turmoil continued.

Suddenly, a feeling of exhaustion came over her and she felt she could go no further. She wandered into the bush beside the road and eventually slumped down under a tree, feeling its strength supporting her back. The trunk was cold and hard. Her head was hot and her hands felt as if they were burning. She wiped them on her skirt. She couldn't breathe. She felt like she was suffocating. The tears came again, and she sobbed until she had no tears left. After some time, she began to wonder where she would spend the night. Just then Edmund appeared and sat down beside her.

"Annie, thank goodness I found you. You can't stay here all night. You must reconsider. Come, I will take you home."

But Annie could only stare at him blankly.

"I can't go home."

Edmund got to his feet.

"Well then, let me take you to Mrs Adam's boarding house. Perhaps you will feel differently in the morning." He helped Annie to her feet and led her to the boarding house where he arranged for a room for her for the night.

Chapter Five

A voice penetrated the fog in Annie's mind. "Hello, what do we have here?"

She looked up and saw two burly police officers who were walking their beat right by where Annie crouched on the footpath.

"What are you doing wandering the streets? Don't you have a home to go to?"

Annie stared at them blankly. Although she had a vague feeling that several days had passed, what had happened in those days was a mystery to her. Around her the city bustled. Horses and carts passed by on the busy streets and the paths thronged with people. She could not remember how she had gotten there. How long had she been in the city? Where had she been staying? None of it was clear to her.

"A home? No ... well, I am not sure."

Annie glanced down at the bag she carried and slowly the memory of her flight from her father's home resurfaced. Thoughts of Edmund and the worry she would have caused him also came to her mind. And what of Father Daly? He would be so angry with her. God would never forgive her sins this time.

"You had better come with us," said the police officer, not unkindly. "What is your name?"

"Annie," she replied.

"Where are you from?"

"I live in Timor at present but my real home is Avoca," she told them.

The police officer looked her up and down. She knew she must look a fright. She patted at her unruly hair, which had escaped the pins that had held it in place. The hem of her dress was dirty from dragging on the ground. How long had she been wandering the streets?

"Well, you are a very long way from home."

"What do you mean? Please, I am not sure where I am. Can you tell me where I am now?"

Annie saw the look of scorn on the police officer's face. But he answered her kindly enough nonetheless.

"You are in Melbourne. Don't you remember coming here? Where have you been staying?"

Annie didn't know what to say. She had no idea where she had been staying. In fact, she had no recollection of how or when she had come to be here. She stared blankly at the police officer.

"I think you will need to come with us. If you do not have anywhere to stay, we can't just leave you here wandering the streets. We will have to charge you with vagrancy."

Soon Annie found herself in a police cell, and her anger had returned with a vengeance.

"What is happening? Why am I locked up in a cell? You must contact my father. His name is Frederick Moore, and he is a mine carpenter at the Grand Duke mine. You must tell him I am here. He will come and get me."

"Calm down, Miss. We will do our best to contact your father." Several days passed and when Frederick did not appear, Annie became more and more withdrawn. Her thoughts turned inward, and she became vague and listless again. Finally, the sergeant of police decided that something had to be done. She couldn't remain in the cells indefinitely. They instigated proceedings for her to be taken before a magistrate.

Annie was confused and did not know what to tell the judge. He asked her several questions for which she had no answer. Finally, he looked at her sympathetically.

"I am sorry, Miss Moore, but as you have no one to look after you, the only option I can see is to have you committed to the Kew Mental Asylum. The doctors have certified that you are of unsound mind, so we have no other alternative." Annie was led out of the court and immediately helped into the police cart.

Now Annie found herself at the gates of a large and imposing building. She looked around in confusion. As the police officers dragged her through the gates and past the gatehouse, the immense proportions of the cement rendered building surrounded by a low brick wall overwhelmed her. The beautifully manicured gardens were in full flower and tall trees surrounded the wall. They continued up the curved driveway towards the front of the building. It was a three-storey building with a mansard roof. To the right and left, the wings of the building stretched out, at the ends of which there were tall towers, also with mansard roofs, topped with cupolas. The police officers led Annie through the arched doorway and into the entrance hallway, where they were met by two female attendants. The smell of bleach assaulted Annie's nostrils.

"Thank you officers, we can take care of Annie from here," said the taller of the two attendants. She was an imposing figure. Middle-aged and dressed in a starched uniform, her hair was tucked up under her cap. She looked at Annie with disdain.

The officers loosened their grip on Annie as the two attendants came to stand on either side of her.

"No, please don't leave me here." During her time in the cell at the police station Annie had begun to feel safe. She had believed that they would bring her father to her to take her home. Now she began to struggle wildly and scream hysterically. But once they were sure that Annie was under control, the two police officers left her to her fate, glad to have completed their duty.

The two attendants led, the by now hysterical, Annie through a door on the left of the building. They entered a passageway, and the attendant, still holding Annie in her firm grip, knocked on another door.

A stern voice called from within the room, bidding them to enter. Annie's eyes darted around the room. The office was small, with little furniture other than a desk and some chairs. Though it was old and had seen much use, the desk was in meticulous order. On it was a quill pen, upright in its stand, an inkwell and an elegant brass letter opener. A shelf behind the desk held several leather-bound books. The office smelt of antiseptic, like a hospital, but Annie could also smell furniture polish and a musty smell of old paper. She looked fearfully at the woman who was sitting behind the desk, writing in a large record book. The office was quiet and still except for the scratch of the pen on the page. The woman looked up from her writing as Annie entered the room and scrutinised her with sharp eyes.

"This is Annie," said the attendant.

"Very well, thank you, Sheila."

"Why am I here?" asked Annie, finding her voice again.

"Please stay calm. Take a seat. We are here to help you," replied the woman behind the desk.

Annie sat down on the hard wooden chair, trembling violently and clutching her bag tightly on her lap.

"You are being admitted to the Kew Lunatic Asylum. My name is Matron Lansdowne."

Annie visibly blanched and her stomach clenched.

"But why am I being admitted? I am not mad," she said. "This is not right. I should not be here." She felt bile rising in her throat as her fear and confusion intensified. She had heard about this place. It was for idiots and inebriates, not the likes of her.

"You are here because you were found wandering the streets with no apparent means of supporting yourself. Your father has been notified and we hope he will be in contact with us soon."

At the mention of her father, Annie felt a strange calmness descend upon her. Surely, he would be here soon to take her home. Although he had been distant and taken little notice of her for years now, she did not think he would allow her to stay in this strange place indefinitely.

"Tell me why you are in Melbourne. You have told the police you live in Timor."

Annie drew in a deep breath. She wanted to stay calm and keep her thoughts clear so that she could tell her story. It was so difficult, as her mind was foggy, and fear seemed to be taking away her power to speak sensibly. In fact, she really could not remember much of what had happened since she had left Edmund at the boarding house. *When was that?* She wondered. She started to speak tentatively.

"Yes, that is correct. At the moment, we live in Timor. But our actual home is in Avoca. My father is working at the mine. I really don't know how I got here. The last thing I remember was leaving my home because nobody there cared about me. I went to a friend for help, but he refused. After that, I don't remember anything. I have been feeling so lost and alone for such a long time now. But I know God is watching me. Perhaps he has sent me here. He is trying to save me. Can you help me?"

"I am sure we can, Annie," said Matron Lansdowne, her voice softening. "But right now, we need to get you settled in. The doctor will need to give you a checkup. Please remove your clothes."

Annie gasped.

"What here? Now?" she said.

"That's right," replied the matron with a frown.

When Annie made no move to undress, the two attendants moved closer and dragged the bag from Annie's tight grip. Then they started to undo the buttons on her bodice.

"You can't take my things. I must have my rosary beads and prayer book!" screamed Annie.

"You will do well not to struggle, Annie," said Matron Lansdowne. "We will go through your things shortly and see what you need to keep with you. Now please undress or the attendants will need to help you."

"Please, no, I cannot."

"But you must. The doctor cannot examine you with your clothing on. You need only remove your outer clothing."

As the attendants tried again to undo the buttons on her bodice, Annie pushed them aside and began to undress herself. Finally, she stood trembling in just her chemise, drawers and stockings.

The doctor was then called. As he entered the room, he pulled his watch from his waistcoat pocket and glanced at it impatiently. The gold watch chain gleamed on his chest.

"This is Doctor Woodforde," said Matron Lansdowne. "He will examine you. Doctor, this is Annie and she has just been brought in by the police."

As he approached Annie, the doctor put his monocle to his eye and peered at her. He was a tall man, impeccably dressed in a three-piece suit over a white starched shirt. His hair was parted sharply on one side and slicked down with brilliantine. His stern face featured a carefully trimmed and waxed moustache.

"Well Annie, what has brought you here?" he asked.

"I don't know why I am here. I have done nothing wrong. I am not mad. It is just that my thoughts are jumbled and I am troubled by them."

"And what thoughts are they, may I ask?"

"I feel God is calling me. I hear voices in my head all the time."

"What are they saying?"

"That I have a duty to God. I must serve him. But it makes me confused because I don't know whether that is what I really want." Annie was not sure why she was telling this stern looking man so much of what was troubling her. For some reason, it was all just tumbling out of her.

"Perhaps you can help me. I feel like a good spirit has brought me here." As Annie fell silent, the doctor took up his stethoscope, and she felt the cold touch of it as he asked her to take deep breaths. He shone a torch in her eyes and conducted several other cursory examinations.

When the examinations were complete he turned to the matron, who took up her pen and dipped it into the inkwell, ready to take notes as he spoke. The scratch of the pen echoed loudly in Annie's head as the matron began to write.

"She is suffering from mania caused by religious excitement. Her bodily state is good, although she is a little feeble. She is reasonably coherent, at the moment, but her memory is obviously impaired. Do you have all that?" When the matron nodded, he left the room abruptly, without another word.

Matron Lansdowne nodded to the attendants who had stood patiently waiting throughout the examination.

"Please take Annie through now so that she can bathe and dress appropriately. Annie, a word of warning. You will do much better here if you remain calm and quiet and try to stay out of trouble." Annie looked vaguely at the matron, not at all sure what she meant. But she picked up her bag and did not resist when the attendants took her by one arm each and led her from the room.

The attendants guided Annie out of the matron's office into the entrance hallway. They walked to the end of the hallway where the attendant, who the matron had called Sheila, pulled out an enormous bunch of keys which were attached to a chain on her belt. She chose one of the larger keys and inserted it into the lock in the sturdy door on the east side of the building. It was the only door which led to the female wing of the asylum. The door swung open to reveal a long corridor. They continued down the corridor towards the dormitories. As they approached the next door Annie heard a loud noise, which increased in volume as they moved closer. Sheila once again reached for her keys and unlocked the door. As the door opened, Annie was taken aback by the scene that confronted her. The crowded room was filled with noise and movement. Shouting and squabbling, raised voices and rebukes from the attendants assaulted her ears. Some among the crowd of women stared vacantly or moaned softly. All the women appeared slumped with furrowed brows. All but a few were dressed in similar attire. The scent of antiseptic and bleach was even stronger here, mixed with the slightly stale odour of many women living together in cramped quarters.

"This is the dayroom," said Sheila loudly, pushing women aside as she led Annie through the throng. Annie cringed. It was too loud, too close. Women crowded in on her as she moved into the room.

Annie was taken into the washroom where she was given a bowl of tepid water, a block of tallow soap and a none too clean cloth. She quickly washed herself, hoping to soon be allowed to dress again. The attendants handed her new clothes, which comprised a shapeless grey dress made from a heavy quilted cotton fabric, underwear, stockings, a calico sunbonnet and large heavy boots.

"But what about my own clothing?"

"No, you must wear the clothing we have given you whilst you are here. Your own belongings will be stored until you need them."

"But my prayer book and rosary beads, I must have them."

"You will be allowed to keep some things. When we get to the dormitory, we will go through your bag and see what you require from it, then we will store your remaining belongings until you need them again."

By this time, Annie was feeling chilled, so she didn't argue further and dressed hastily. The attendants laced up the leather thongs that held the dress together at the back.

Once Annie was dressed she picked up her bag again, and the attendants guided her through to the dormitory where she would sleep. They walked through several dormitories, each one having to be unlocked as they went, until they reached the one where Annie would sleep. The long room had a high ceiling and a polished timber floor. The walls were painted yellow, perhaps in an attempt to make the room appear sunny and bright. There were framed prints on the walls, but otherwise no decoration. The dormitory was sparsely furnished with rows of iron bedsteads which were raised only a few inches from the floor. The beds were all neatly made and covered with check bedspreads. A wooden chair stood beside each bed. There was a fireplace set with kindling and logs ready to be lit. It was surrounded by a guard, which Annie could see was locked with a sturdy padlock.

"This will be your bed," said the quieter of the two attendants, not unkindly. "You may rest here for a few minutes, but then you must join the others in the dayroom."

Annie looked around her. Although the dormitory was crowded with beds, little more than two feet separating them from each other, it looked clean and tidy. There were windows along one side emitting plenty of light on this sunny day.

"Now Annie, please unpack your bag. We will need to decide what you may keep and what will need to be stored."

Annie put her bag on the bed and began to unpack. The attendants bundled all her clothes into a neat pile. Although she pleaded to keep her things, she was only allowed to hold on to her bible and rosary beads. She wondered vaguely what had happened to her small amount of savings that she had brought with her. But she still could not recall the time she had supposedly spent wandering the streets of Melbourne. So perhaps she had spent it all.

Annie put her prayer book and rosary beads back into her bag, grateful that she had been allowed to keep them. Then she pushed the bag under the bed as directed by the attendants.

Sheila was impatient. Although the other attendant had said Annie might rest for a minute, Sheila had other ideas. After only a few moments, she hustled Annie out of the dormitory towards the day room.

As they entered the room, Annie was once again assaulted by the noise and chaos. Fear rose in her throat. She grabbed at the sleeve of the kinder attendant.

"Please, you can't leave me here, I shouldn't be in this place."

Sheila turned and grabbed Annie's arm and dragged her away from the attendant.

"Do not lay hands on an attendant or you will be restrained. Of course you are meant to be here, you silly girl. You will just have to make the most of it."

With that both attendants left her alone and moved about the dayroom seeing to the other women. The women began to gather around Annie, reaching out to touch her, playing with her hair. Annie realised her naturally unruly hair would long ago have escaped her loose chignon and she would now look quite a fright. Annie tried not to show her fear as she shrunk back from the women.

Once the novelty of having a newcomer in their midst had worn off, the women left Annie alone, she found a chair and sat huddled in despair. She tried to recall all that had happened but she really had no clear idea of what had led her here. Eventually she was able to summon the energy to raise her head to survey her surroundings. The room seemed to hold some comforts. There was a large bowl of flowers on a table in the corner, and Annie noticed a small bookcase. Once again, there was a fireplace surrounded by a sturdy guard. She also noticed a battered old piano in the corner. She vaguely wondered if she would be allowed to play it. Her music had been important to her over the years. Sitting at the piano, feeling the ivory of the keys and playing the music of her favourite composers had calmed her mind when her confusion and anxiety had been at their worst. But that too had been ripped away from her when the family had moved to Timor. Her beloved piano had been left at the house in Avoca.

As she became more accustomed to the noise, Annie realised that some of the patients seemed quite calm. One woman was even sitting quietly embroidering, and a few were reading newspapers and books. However, most of the women appeared blank and listless. As she looked more closely at the women around her, she noticed that several of them were wearing strange canvas garments, with leather straps buckled at the back. The patient's hands appeared to be locked into the pockets. She cringed at the sight, wondering how the women coped wearing those dreadful garments. They would not even be able to scratch themselves.

It was, by this time, late afternoon. A bell began to ring loudly. Annie looked around in alarm but soon realised that the patients were being chivvied along to make their way to the dining area where tea was to be served. Long deal tables were set up, surrounded by high-backed forms where the women sat. The meal consisted of bread and butter washed down with tea. It was not very appetising, and the bread felt like sawdust in Annie's mouth. Although she suddenly realised she was hungry, she struggled to eat.

After the meal, the women made their way back to the washroom, where they washed and got ready for bed. They all changed into nightwear in the dayroom, and put their clothes into cupboards before they returned to their dormitories. Those who were clad in the canvas garments were shepherded into single rooms off to the side of the dormitories. Annie peeked in as she walked past and could see that the rooms were tiny, much like the cell that she had spent time in at the police station. The attendants emerged from these rooms carrying the canvas garments and locked the doors behind them. The oil lanterns in the wall sconces shone dully on the yellow walls as darkness descended. Once all the women were in their beds, the lights were extinguished and the dormitory door was locked.

Annie heard the rasping sound of the key turning in the lock and finally she let her guard down and wept quietly into her pillow. She lay on her thin straw mattress, waiting for sleep to transport her away from this nightmare. She still had no idea why they had brought her here. But she could only hope that her father would come for her soon. She wept quietly until she could cry no more, and in her exhaustion, she fell into a fitful slumber.

Chapter Six

Elsie Lansdowne revelled in the long walk home to her lodgings. Most nights she was required to stay in her small cell-like room at the asylum. Actually, it was not a cell in the true sense of the word because, unlike the inmates, she was not locked in and was free to move about the asylum if she pleased. When she was not required to stay, she savoured the opportunity to escape the misery of her workplace.

From the high vantage point of the asylum, Elsie could glimpse the tall city buildings off in the distance as she walked towards the gates. She always left via the front gates rather than the shorter route through the rear because it gave her the opportunity to walk through the bush and along the curved track beside the part of the Yarra River that the locals had christened Yarra Bends. The water glistened in the sunlight as the river twisted and turned, carving a path through the surrounding countryside.

As she walked, Elsie thought about the newest inmate, Annie. What was it about her? For some reason, Elsie felt an affinity with the young girl. Perhaps she reminded Elsie of her own daughter, Viola. Yes, that was probably it. Annie was a little older than her daughter had been, but somehow, she seemed younger and more naïve. Chances were she had not had to endure the same trials growing up as Viola had at the hands of her cruel father.

The early autumn evening was hot, but as she approached the river, she felt the cool breeze blowing off the water. Bird song replaced the raucous noise of the women squabbling in the yards. It was always cooler down here by the river. The sharp, minty scent of eucalyptus emanating from the gum trees caught in her nostrils. Elsie loved this sensation because it cleared away the memory of the potent smell of bleach and other unpleasant human smells that filled the asylum. Gum trees lined the banks of the river where they had flourished for hundreds of years.

Soon she turned left away from the river up towards the village of Kew, where she lived. Leaving the peace of the riverbank, she entered the noisome, malodorous streets. People were leaving their places of work and making their way home along the roughly made streets with their stinking open gutters. Even though the Melbourne city streets now had underground sewers, it was not so in Kew, where the waste ran in the open drains and on into the river. Elsie stopped at the grocery store and purchased some milk for her cup of tea and some vegetables from the market gardener. She then moved onto the butcher's shop, which gave off its own particular odour from the meat hanging in the open. Here she purchased a small piece of mutton for the stew that she would make for her evening meal. She had been late leaving the asylum after admitting Annie and finishing up her reports. Already the lamplighter was making his way down the street, lighting the gas streetlights. Elsie turned left again into her own small side street and felt a sense of relief wash over her.

She inserted the key into the lock and twisted it until she heard a satisfying click. Taking a deep breath, she pushed open the door to her sanctuary, a small single-storey terrace house. The door opened onto a long hallway with rooms off to the left. The front room, her bedroom, then the dining room and finally her small kitchen and washroom area at the back. She stepped inside and put her hat and gloves on the lacquered hall table before walking down the hallway to the kitchen.

She lived alone but was glad to do so. It was peaceful, and she did not need to think of anyone but herself for a blessed time. Her husband had died some years ago, but she did not mourn him. He had been a cruel and heartless man who had made her and her daughter's life hell on earth.

She gathered a handful of kindling from the woodpile in the tiny backyard. Back inside she laid the kindling across the grate of the cast iron stove and struck a match, watching as the flames licked against the wood and caught hold. Then she carefully added some larger pieces of wood. The room was sparsely furnished with a small wooden table and three rickety wooden chairs. The sideboard held her precious but sparse collection of crockery and a couple of pots hung over the stove. She filled the kettle and placed it back on the stove, its permanent position, so that whenever the fire was alight, there would be hot water available. The fire in the stove had been out for some days as she had been staying at the asylum so the room was uncharacteristically but pleasantly cool. She felt the warmth from the stove begin to permeate the kitchen. The room would soon be uncomfortably hot so she hurriedly cut up her meat and vegetables. Her stew was bubbling away on the wood stove in no time.

Once that was done, she allowed herself the luxury of a small glass of sherry. She reached up into the cupboard above her small ice chest and retrieved the bottle. The cork made a satisfying pop as she pulled it from the bottle and the aroma of the alcohol was pleasant as she poured it into a small glass. She had never partaken of alcohol whilst her husband was alive. He drank enough for both of them. But now, knowing that she controlled the amount of alcohol she drank and not the other way round, she was comforted by the feeling of relaxation that came over her. She felt the slight burn of the sherry in her throat as she swallowed.

After checking that her stew was simmering away gently, she took her glass of sherry and went into her front room which was still pleasantly cool. As she lit the gas lantern it cast a warm glow over the room. A weary sigh escaped Elsie as she sat heavily in her favourite chair. She enjoyed the feeling of being home surrounded by her favorite possessions, with no responsibilities to think about, at least for the next few hours.

In stark contrast to the sparsely furnished kitchen, this room was a cosy haven decorated with her favourite possessions. Since her husband had died and she had returned to the job she loved as a nurse, she had been able to afford some small luxuries for this room. Apart from her comfortable chintz-covered armchair, there was a beautiful chaise lounge and two small side tables featuring some of Elsie's precious ornaments. Among her other possessions was her collection of books stacked neatly in the bookcase. Elsie was an avid reader. Books such as *Jane Eyre* and *Pride and Prejudice* were her usual choice, but she was very much looking forward to reading the latest mystery by Arthur Conan Doyle, which she had recently acquired.

The coal scuttle was full beside the open cast iron fireplace which was set with kindling ready to light, as the cooler nights would undoubtedly be just around the corner. Elsie did not like the cold winter months and was always well prepared. On the mantelpiece which topped the timber surround of the fireplace was a photo of a pretty young girl, her daughter. She missed Viola more than words could describe. Her short life had been a joy to Elsie and when her husband was not around, the two of them had enjoyed reading together and laughed joyously at amusing stories in the newspapers of the day. They had knitted and sewn needlepoint, both having a love of the finer things in life. But her daughter's life had been cruelly cut short. It didn't bear thinking about. Elsie twisted the thin gold band on the ring finger of her left hand. Despite now being free of her cruel husband, she still wore her wedding ring. Often she wondered why, but she never felt able to remove it.

Elsie slowly sipped her sherry and the outside world slipped away as the wine relaxed her and she forgot the trials of the day. However, she could not stop her mind from going back to Annie. The poor girl probably did not need to be locked away from the world. When the police had brought her in, she was completely distraught and Elsie could certainly understand why they had brought her to the asylum. But Elsie knew from experience that with some support from her family, Annie might have been spared from being committed. Now it would be some time before the treatments would have any effect on her mania. But what could Elsie do? The doctors and superintendents rarely listened to advice from the nurses. Even though Elsie held a position of some authority in the women's section of the asylum, her male counterparts held the power and made all the decisions about who would stay and who might one day leave. There were few that left, thought Elsie ruefully.

As the alcohol seeped into her blood, she relaxed still more. She really must get up soon and check her stew. Her stomach rumbled as she felt the first pangs of hunger and dragged herself to her feet. She ate the stew in the small kitchen and washed the dishes. Then she made herself a cup of tea and went back to the front room. She sat down again and took a book from her bookcase. It was one she had read many times, but she found it relaxing to read before bed. Soon her eyelids were drooping, so she picked up the lantern and made her way to her cosy bedroom. It had been a long few days at the asylum and soon she was drifting off to sleep.

Chapter Seven

Morning dawned on the first day of Annie's incarceration. The day started early with the ringing of bells. Annie woke with a start not understanding where she was. She looked around her at the rows of beds and the women emerging from them. Suddenly the previous day's events came flooding back to her and she began to panic. Her chest tightened, she felt paralysed. Attendants unlocked the doors and moved around the room, calling for the inmates to get up. The blinds were thrown up and the windows were opened just a crack to expose the sunrise and to let in some fresh air. Annie felt a dull ache in her head as she tried to lift it from the pillow. She looked out at the bright autumn day. It was some comfort to see the world outside the dormitory. She imagined everyone awakening in her country home. The house would be rowdy as the children got out of bed, did their morning chores and then the family would sit down together for breakfast.

The women were slow to move and were prodded and poked until they eventually, wearily, rose from their beds. Annie felt groggy and dazed. Her sleep had been filled with strange dreams of home, and she did not feel at all refreshed. She dragged herself from the bed and went to find her clothes, which were all piled together in cupboards in the dayroom. Women squabbled over who belonged to which garment so that Annie wasn't at all sure that she managed to find the clothes she had worn yesterday. The heavy cotton dress she eventually put on had a faint odour of perspiration. She wondered again why she couldn't just wear her own clothes. She was then directed into the crowded wash-room where the women were once again required to wash. One attendant was on duty, armed with a brush and comb to tame the unruly locks of the patients. Once they were dressed, the women stripped their beds so that they could take the bedding out to air. They were then provided with brooms, buckets and mops to sweep and wash the floor. Once the attendants were satisfied that everything was in order the women were led to the dining area. Breakfast comprised bread and butter and tea. For the epileptics who might choke, the bread was broken up and mixed with the tea. A portion of the sop was served to each in a tin pannikin. The attendants mingled with the women, assisting those who could not feed themselves.

Annie noticed that after breakfast, once the dishes had been cleared, the attendants became more vigilant and made an effort to quieten the women.

Soon the doctor, who had examined Annie the day before, entered the room with Matron Lansdowne. They proceeded to inspect the dayroom and dormitories to ensure that everything was in order. The doctor checked some of the patients and prescribed extra diet and other medicinal aids such as port or brandy, sago and beef tea for those who were thought to be sickly.

With the major work for the day over, the women were herded out into the yard. It was another warm day, so they all donned their calico sun bonnets.

Despite the pounding of her head and the tightness in her chest Annie was glad to be out in the open air. Although she was not at all sure of her surroundings as she stumbled out into the yard she breathed deeply, filling her lungs with the fresh, warm air, and looked towards the sky. It was good to feel the sun on her face. Being a country girl she felt calmer outside and eventually her breathing settled and she began admiring the garden around her. It was a picturesque garden. There were orderly rows of shrubs and flower beds, but she noticed they were coming to the end of their summer best.

She began to take more notice of the other women and studied them surreptitiously from under the brim of her bonnet. Some strolled listlessly around the circular pathway, muttering to themselves. One woman was not making use of the pathway. She walked a short distance, then turned and walked back the way she had come. She repeated this process over and over, wearing a pathway in the overgrown grass area. Other women walked in pairs and chatted to each other.

As Annie became accustomed to her immediate surroundings, she looked further afield. She could see the large Moreton Bay fig and Cyprus trees that surrounded the area outside the walls. And behind them again she could glimpse the natural bush with gum trees, she-oaks and acacias. Her gaze was drawn even further afield to the ranges beyond. These pleasant views of the outside world drew her attention to the brick wall that enclosed the garden. She could easily see out over the wall. However, she then noticed the slope of the grassed area down to the wall. From the bottom of the wide sloping trench, she could see that the wall was at least ten feet high. She assumed this was a means to stop inmates from scaling the wall and escaping.

Suddenly, she was startled out of her reverie as one of the women fell into step beside her. Her breath came short and sharp as she wondered what this woman wanted with her.

"Hello," said the woman kindly. "My name is Helena. You are new, aren't you?"

Annie relaxed a little as she looked at the kindly face. "Yes," replied Annie. "I haven't been here long." Annie tried to think how long she had been here but she wasn't at all sure.

"My name is Annie." Annie looked at Helena, quite surprised that she seemed calm and definitely did not look mad or in any way disturbed. Annie was confused. Whilst she did feel a little out of sorts and was missing some details of the recent past, she felt she should not be locked up here and it seemed to her that she was not the only one. Many of the women seemed calm and sensible, certainly not raving lunatics beating their heads against the wall, as she previously had imagined people incarcerated in an institution such as this would be.

"I won't be here long though," continued Annie. "My father will be here to get me soon."

Helena smiled sadly. "I pray that is true."

The two women continued to pace around the yard without further conversation for some time. They passed a young woman crumbling a crust of bread to feed to the birds. She must have saved it from her breakfast. Annie wondered at her generosity to the birds. There was little enough to eat. Annie's stomach was already rumbling.

As they continued to walk, Annie became curious.

"Why are you here?" she asked.

"I don't really know," said Helena. "Apparently I am a danger to myself."

Annie looked at her questioningly. Helena seemed to be in complete control. She changed the subject.

"I have just noticed the strange way the ground slopes down to the wall."

"Yes," replied Helena. "I am told they are called 'ha ha' walls. It is so the appearance from outside is of a benevolent and welcoming place for we lunatics and inebriates to be held. The walls appear only to be a few feet high from the outside. But as you can see, they are very high on this side, which of course prevents anyone from escaping."

A bell rang again, and the attendants herded all the women back into the dining area for dinner. The attendants bought in enormous platters of roasted meat which they proceeded to carve. They served this with potatoes. Annie glanced around at the plates of meat as the women started to eat. Some meals looked more appetising than others, depending on the cuts of meat they had received. Annie's portion was fatty and grisly. Still, she was hungry, so she attempted to force the food down.

After they had eaten, they made their way out into the yards, where they spent the rest of the day. The afternoon dragged leaving nothing for Annie to do but get lost in her thoughts. She had been used to being so busy looking after the children and seeing to the other chores at home that she barely had time to think. She was relieved when the bells rang again to signal that tea was served. The meal once again consisted of bread and butter with weak, watery tea.

When they were all getting ready for bed, Annie once again noticed the woman with her needlework. She sat on the edge of her bed, intent on the small, neat stitches she was forming on the little square of calico. The woman saw Annie staring.

"What are you looking at girlie?" said the woman.

"Oh, I am sorry," said Annie. "I didn't mean to stare. I just wondered how you can sit so calmly and sew amongst all this racket."

"It keeps me sane. I am Catherine. What's your name?"

"I am Annie," she replied. "But I shouldn't be here. I am not mad."

The woman grinned. "Well, if you are not mad now, you soon will be." She cackled loudly at her own joke. Annie did not think it was funny and moved away from the woman. It was time for bed and the attendants were moving around the room, urging the more infirm of the women to hurry and get into bed. Annie slipped into bed and pulled the blanket over her head and once again began to sob softly. Although she had only survived her first day here, it felt like an eternity. She longed to go home.

The days passed by in a tortured blur; Annie's mind was plagued with restless thoughts as she awoke each morning and shakily pulled herself out of bed, the cold reality that she was still locked away in the asylum settling in like a heavy fog. Where was her father? He should have been here to collect her by now. Annie loved her father, but she had to admit that since her mother had died, he had taken much less interest in her. But she did not believe that he would leave her here. He must come soon.

"Oh Helena, when is my father going to come?" The two women were once again walking together in the yard. "I don't know how much longer I can cope with this."

"Annie, you haven't any choice. You must try to stay calm. You know what will happen if you don't," replied Helena.

"What do you mean? What will happen?"

"You will be restrained and locked in a single cell."

Annie was horrified at the thought of being locked away on her own.

"Yes, but that won't happen to me. I am not a lunatic."

"Perhaps, but you are here and there is no escape."

"You don't think my father is coming do you?"

"I am really very sorry, Annie. But no, I don't think he is coming. You need to accept that."

"You are wrong. I can't stay here. I am not mad. My father will come for me." Annie felt herself becoming agitated and there was a familiar tightness in her chest.

"Calm down. I don't think you are mad, Annie, but if you are angry and violent, then you will be considered a lunatic."

But Annie was not convinced. Each day, she asked at least one of the attendants whether there was any word from her father. This morning, she had asked to speak with Matron Lansdowne when she came to inspect the dormitory.

Annie followed her around.

"Please Matron, may I speak with you?" she asked. But Matron Lansdowne would not be interrupted.

"I am sorry Annie, I am very busy. I do not have time."

"But my father. You said that my father was coming to collect me."

"I have not heard anything. You will need to be patient. If your father is coming, he will be here in due course."

Annie grabbed desperately at the sleeve of the matron's gown. "Please, you must help me. I should not be in here!"

Annie was immediately restrained by Sheila and the other attendant who was assisting Matron Lansdowne on her rounds, and she continued her inspection.

Annie's face grew red.

"Let me go," she cried as she struggled against the attendants.

"Calm down Annie," said Sheila. "You won't do yourself any favours by becoming angry."

"But I need to find out when my father is coming."

"When he comes you will know about it."

As Matron Lansdowne finished her inspection the attendants relaxed their grip on Annie. Annie collapsed to the floor, and the attendants left her to her sorrows. One of the women approached Annie and tried to console her. But Annie lashed out.

"Leave me alone," she said, pushing the other woman violently so that she stumbled and almost fell. The attendants were immediately on the scene again, holding Annie in a tight grip.

"Let me go," she cried.

"Calm down Annie, or we will have to restrain you," said Sheila. "I am sure you have seen the camisoles on some of the inmates, with their hands locked into the pockets. They are the ones who have had serious breakdowns and have completely lost control. They spend most of their time in isolation in the single cells and are only allowed out briefly for some exercise. That is where you will end up if you are not careful."

This caused Annie to pause, remembering Helena's words and thinking about those poor women whom she had seen walking around the yard in camisoles. She breathed deeply to calm herself. It seemed that the staff here at the asylum were not going to help her. Helena was soon at her side as they proceeded with the others out into the yard.

"Annie, what is wrong?" said Helena. "You must try to control yourself. You will alienate the attendants if you continue to lose your temper. It does not take much for them to find an excuse to send you to the refractory ward."

"What is that?" asked Annie.

"It is where violent or misbehaving patients are sent. You would be restrained and put into isolation in one of the single cells. You don't want that, do you?"

Annie was shocked. "No, of course I don't. But why won't they tell me when father is coming?"

Helena looked at Annie with concern and tried again.

"Are you sure he is coming for you?" she asked gently.

Annie had to admit she was not entirely sure.

"Oh Helena, I can't be sure. I feel like my life is over. I have actually not had much of a life since my mother died. Before that we were such a happy family. Father was always so patient and told wonderful stories."

Chapter Eight

Annie's father, Frederick Moore, was the local butcher in the bustling mining town of Avoca. Annie loved to visit his butcher shop on the main street of town. When there was shopping to be done Annie would walk with her mother and her six older brothers and sisters, down the wide main street. The family lived in a large two-storey brick home on the banks of the Avoca River. The town had prospered greatly during the halcyon days of the gold rush and stately buildings such as the Avoca Hotel, the courthouse, and post office lined the main street. The road was divided into two carriageways with a line of trees running down the middle. Annie loved the hustle and bustle of the busy town. Now that farms were cropping up everywhere on the land surrounding the town, Annie would watch entranced as the bullock teams passed, carrying their loads of wool and crops to the markets. Although the ground was rocky, the dark soil was rich and loamy. The farmers made good use of the rocks as they cleared the land, using them to build fences and shepherds' huts. In the spring, the crops waved in the wind and there would be a flurry of activity as the farmers harvested their crops and the large flocks of sheep were shorn.

Although the gold rush had been over for many years, gold mining was still going on in the area, but now it was being carried out by large mining companies who were drilling deep into the earth to find the gold reefs that lay below. Annie's father was a carpenter by trade so apart from the butchery, he also worked in the deep mines shoring up the shafts with timber.

Sometimes, when they were out shopping, they would call into the butcher shop. It was a bit gruesome seeing all the carcasses hanging from the butcher's hooks. The shop smelled strongly of freshly cut meat. It always amazed Annie how quickly her father carved up the meat. He would take his knife from the pouch that hung on a belt around his waist and sharpen it on a stone. Then he would take a carcass from the hook, throw it on the huge wooden block in the middle of the shop and carve off a leg. When he came to the bones, he would take out his cleaver and chop through them.

Each evening when their father came home from work and the evening meal was eaten and the dishes washed, the children gathered around their father's comfortable chair and Annie, being the baby of the family although she was nearly five years old, would crawl into his lap. Frederick was a tall, distinguished looking man. He had a full beard, which Annie liked to run her fingers through. His deep brown eyes would look at her fondly. In the evenings, after his day's work at the butcher shop, he always found time for the children.

"Tell us the story about the troopers, Father," said Annie.

Her father smiled at her and the other children. Fortunately, he never tired of telling this story.

"Well, now that was a day," he began. "It was a long time ago when gold could be picked up off the ground. Can you imagine that? Big chunks of gold, if you were lucky enough to find one. But the miners were unhappy. They all had to purchase a miner's license for a good deal of money."

At this point, Annie piped up.

"How much, Father?"

"One whole pound. That's a lot of money, isn't it?" Frederick continued with the story.

"So, of course, not all the miners could afford to pay the license fee. Only the lucky ones who found gold. When the troopers came along to check that all the miners held licenses, the miners without licenses would try to hide from the troopers. But eventually they got tired of the greedy government and the harsh treatment by the troopers. So, they gathered timber from the mines and built a stockade. They armed themselves with any weapons they could find. The blacksmiths made steel pikes they attached to sturdy poles fashioned from tree branches. Some had guns, but many had only their handmade weapons. The troopers got word of the protest and there was a big riot." This part of the story was deliciously scary to Annie.

"The troopers attacked the gold diggers. Some of the miners were killed, but some were able to escape. So, the troopers tried to track them down. I was carting goods to the gold fields that very day when the troopers rode up and bailed me up. They searched my cart in case the gold diggers were hiding under the canvas amongst the goods. Of course, they found nothing, so I went on my way."

Annie's mother Ellen sat opposite in her comfortable chair, quietly working on her needlepoint as Frederick recited the story yet again. She was a gentle and fragile Irish Catholic immigrant. Her early life had been harsh. At one time she had been imprisoned in a Belfast jail having being convicted of vagrancy. Born in 1834 in Tipperary, she somehow survived the potato famine to come to Australia as a bounty immigrant in 1854 and spent the first few years working in St Kilda for Dr Van Hornet. He had been kind to her, but when she met and married Frederick, she knew true happiness for the first time in her life. She was a small woman with hazel eyes and long, shiny dark hair, which she wore pinned high on top of her head. It was a mixed marriage, as Frederick was a protestant. But there was never any doubt that they loved each other very much. There was never a cross word between them.

When the children weren't listening to their father's stories, the family would gather around the piano in the drawing room. Ellen played Irish ballads and the family would sing along as she played. She taught them all to play, but not all the children were as keen as Annie. Even though she was the youngest and not yet five, she took every opportunity to sit at the piano and practice. She knew this pleased her mother, and she wanted nothing more than to make her mother and father happy.

Annie also loved to help her mother around the house. Their house was more like a mansion compared to the other homes on the street. Frederick often reminded the family how lucky they were that he had been able to purchase a pair of fine strong horses and a sturdy dray when he first came to Australia. Many people found wealth digging for gold, but many did not. Frederick had discovered very early on that there was money to be made carting goods to the goldfields.

The parlour was Annie's favorite room with its red velvet curtains and soft, fluffy cushions. She took great pleasure and care when her mother allowed her to dust this room. Although she couldn't reach the mantelpiece, she made sure that there was never any dust to be seen on the side tables and book cases. She had to be very careful when she dusted the delicate ornaments.

When her mother was baking, Annie would pull up a stool beside the bench and stir the mixture with a wooden spoon. Sometimes her mother even allowed her to crack the eggs into the mixture.

Every Sunday morning Ellen Moore would make sure all her children were dressed in their Sunday best with shiny clean faces and hands and hair combed. They would all climb into the cart to take the short journey to the catholic church to attend Mass. The church was a solemn place with its high ceilings and soft candle lighting. They all filed into the pew and Annie always tried to sit next to her mother. The priest's fiery sermon would reverberate through the congregation. Annie found the priest very scary and snuggled into her mother's side. He preached about going to hell and told the congregation that if they sinned, they would face eternal damnation. Annie was not really certain what this meant, but it certainly sounded extremely scary.

Annie loved all her brothers and sisters, but her favourite was Cora. Cora was only two years older than Annie, and the two were inseparable.

"Cora, will you come outside and play?" said Annie. "It is such a sunny day. I can hear the frogs croaking down by the river."

"Oh yes please," said Cora. "Can we please Mummy?"

"You may, but you must keep an eye on Annie, Cora. And do not go near the river."

The Avoca River ran past their home on the other side of the road. In winter, after heavy rains, it flowed strongly and provided plenty of water, which was an important resource in any mining town.

The two girls ran from the house, leaving the rest of their brothers and sisters to their own devices. They loved to play on their own.

It was a lovely spring day, and the paddocks were covered with daisies. Cora and Annie sat amongst the yellow flowers and Cora showed Annie how to make daisy chains. Annie found it difficult, with her tiny fingers, to split the stem of a daisy and thread another daisy through. But soon they were both adorned with daisy chain necklaces, bracelets and crowns. Then they wandered down close to the river, but Cora remembered her mother's warning.

"Annie, we mustn't go too close. You know I am supposed to look after you."

Annie frowned. "Just a bit further. The frogs are making such a racket today. I love to hear them. I wonder if there are any tadpoles."

"Well, perhaps we can ask father to come down with us so we can catch some later."

They heard their mother calling from the house.

"It is time for tea. Hurry or you will miss out."

The two girls wasted no time in returning to the house. After being outside in the fresh air for all that time, they were ravenous.

On school days, the children would all walk to school together. They did not have far to go, only about a mile. Other children had much farther to walk from farms in the outlying areas. Annie could not contain her happiness when finally she was old enough to go to school. For a long time she had sat at the kitchen window and watched her brothers and sisters head off each day wishing that she could go too. But finally, she turned five and her turn came. The school was a big imposing building with a turret-like roof. To Annie it looked like a castle from one of the fairy storybooks she liked to read. Although the teachers were strict, Annie loved school and learned quickly. She loved reading and was soon reading books like those that the older children were reading. Her other favourite pastime at school was music. She sang loudly and cheerfully whenever she had the chance.

It all happened very suddenly. An unnatural silence settled over the house. Ellen was very unwell and the children were urged to be quiet so as not to disturb her. The Doctor came frequently to care for their sick mother.

After one visit by the Doctor, Annie's older brother Howard was called to his father's study. Annie and Cora were both horrified that their mother, who was always so bright and cheery, was suddenly so unwell. They peered in at the door of the study to try to find out what was going on.

"Howard, the Doctor has ordered a tonic for your mother," said Frederick. "I do not want to leave her alone. You will have to go to the apothecary to get the prescription that the Doctor has ordered."

"Of course, father," said Howard, taking the scrap of paper his father proffered. It was covered with the Doctor's scrawl, which meant nothing to Howard. As he was about to leave the room, Frederick spotted Annie and Cora by the door.

"Take Annie and Cora with you," he said. "They could do with a walk and some fresh air." He smiled affectionately at the two little girls, but soon the smile slipped back into the worried frown that the children were becoming used to.

Howard left the room.

"Come on you two. Don't dilly dally. Get your bonnets. We need to be quick."

Annie was pleased to be included in this important mission and stood patiently whilst Cora tied the ribbons of her bonnet under her chin.

The three children were soon walking down the road towards the bridge. It was not a long walk, but Howard was impatient and hurried them along. The girls had to run to keep up with him.

Soon they arrived at the Prescription Depot, where the apothecary was busily mixing a potion behind the counter. As they entered the shop, Annie looked around her. It was the first time she had been inside the little store and she was astounded by the rows of shelves neatly arranged with jars containing all types of herbs and chemicals that the apothecary used to make salves, potions and balms to sooth or cure people's ailments.

"Hello young people," said the apothecary. "What can I do for you?"

"My mother is very ill," said Howard. "The Doctor has prescribed a tonic."

He handed over the scrawled note from the Doctor.

"Ah yes, I can see that will be most efficacious in the treatment of your poor mother's ailment. It will take me a few moments to prepare it."

The children watched on as the apothecary took several jars from the shelves and measured portions of each into a smaller jar. Soon the tonic was ready. Howard handed over the payment and the children were on their way.

Howard hurried into his father's study as soon as they arrived home. Frederick took the tonic and went upstairs to Ellen's room to administer it. The children prayed it would help their mother to get better.

But alas, the tonic and the other treatments that the Doctor prescribed did little and Ellen did not improve. Frederick was morose and had little time for the children. The older children had to manage the household, cooking the meals and cleaning. Annie did what she could to help, still hoping that her mother would soon be well again.

Annie and the other children were only allowed into her sickroom for a few minutes at a time. They would creep into her room and sit quietly by her bed. She was so pale and listless. Often, she was too ill to speak to them and sometimes she would not even open her eyes. But one day when Annie and Cora were sitting by her bed, she opened her eyes and smiled gently.

"My two baby girls. You look so pretty sitting there. But what sad faces. Don't you have a smile for your poor mother?"

"Oh, but mother, you are not going to die are you?" asked Cora, who was seven years old and thought she was wise in the ways of the world.

"Don't talk such silly nonsense, Cora. Of course not."

Annie felt only slightly convinced by this. Not that she really understood about death, like Cora did. But she tried to smile for her mother. Soon their father came and shooed them out of the room so that he could sit with their mother.

Annie and Cora prayed endlessly for their mother to get better. Every evening Annie would get out her tiny leather bound, gold embossed prayer book with its wafer-thin pages and with the help of her sister, she would say her prayers. Together they knelt by their bed and recited the Act of Contrition and The Lord's Prayer. They finished their prayers by asking God to make their mother well again.

But unfortunately, it was to no avail and their mother continued to get worse until eventually she passed away quietly and with a minimum of fuss, much as she had always done in life. Everyone was heartbroken. Annie did not completely understand what had happened, but she just knew that her mother was no longer there. Strange goings-on were happening in the house. For one thing, all the mirrors had been covered with black cloths and there was a large black wreath on the front door.

Their mother had been laid out in the parlour for several days. Annie had only been allowed into the parlour once. Her father had gathered the children together.

"Now children, you must say goodbye to your mother," he said quietly. The grief was clear in the lines of his face. The children, the younger ones in particular, feared what they would see when they entered the room.

Branches of rosemary and large vases of flowers created a sickly-sweet fragrance designed to disguise the odour of death that was emanating from their poor mother.

One by one, the children filed by their mother and said good-bye. The older children leaned down to gently kiss her cold cheek. Annie was too small to see above the table, so Howard lifted her so that she could see and touch her mother. But Annie recoiled. The pale figure looked nothing like her mother. She could not touch her and was glad when she left the room. But as she left the room, she burst into tears and sobbed inconsolably.

"Where is Mother? That can't be her. She is so white and what has happened to her lovely red lips?"

"Come Annie," said Annie's older sister, leading her away from her father. Annie could see the tears in his eyes as she was led away.

Over the next few days, relations and friends visited to pay their respects, but now the day of the funeral was upon them.

It was a hot summer day with dark clouds in the west threatening a thunderstorm. Annie and the other children were dressed in black mourning garb. Annie clutched at the high stiff collar of the black crepe dress that she wore. It was identical to the ones her sisters wore. It was tight and uncomfortable. She had been told that they would need to wear black clothes for several months until the mourning period was over. Annie grimaced at the thought. She stared at her father. He looked sad and stern in his black suit and black necktie and gloves. She had watched from the doorway of the parlour as they had placed her mother in a wooden coffin and loaded it onto the funeral cart, for the journey to the cemetery. The family followed along riding in a cart driven by her father's close friend. Family and friends surrounded the grave as Father Daly performed the graveside service. Annie noticed that only the family wore black. The Moore family were well known and respected and Ellen had been well liked by the townsfolk so there was a large crowd in attendance, all dressed in their Sunday best. Annie stood close to her father, trying to hold back tears as their mother's coffin was lowered into the ground. Cora reached out and took Annie's hand and they each took a handful of dirt and threw it onto the coffin as their father and older siblings had done. As the priest said the final prayers, they all said their last goodbyes and returned to the house, where everyone gathered for refreshments and to remember Ellen.

Frederick was inconsolable. He did not go to work for several days but rather sat in his study looking morose. Each evening, the children would enter his study and Annie would try to sit on his knee and ask him to tell them a story. But after a few moments, he would push her away and chase them all from the room. It seemed he had no time for any of them. He just became more and more withdrawn.

Annie and Cora tried to cheer him up. They both continued to practice playing the piano, hoping that the music would please their father. He had always joined in when their mother had played the piano and they had all gathered around to sing. Although Annie was young, she had an aptitude for music and her playing became quite proficient. But none of it seemed to help. On some occasions, Frederick would angrily tell them to stop playing. When this happened, they would both leave the room silently, hoping not to anger him further.

Annie grew sadder as her father's mood did not improve. The children relied on each other for comfort. Each night Annie and Cora would take out their prayer books and say prayers for their departed mother. Annie took out her pen and ink and with Cora's help wrote her mother's name followed by the date of her death in the flyleaf of the little prayer book in her very best hand.

Chapter Nine

Annie had to grow up quickly in the four years after her mother died. Whilst her father went about his work at the butcher shop and the mine, he took little interest in home life. The children had to fend for themselves and Annie tried to do her fair share. Her oldest sister made sure there was food on the table. How they had all managed was a mystery to Annie. But now Frederick had brought another woman into their home.

"Children, I would like you to meet my friend Lillie. We are going to be married and she will be your new mother. They are generally well behaved, Lillie," he said in an aside to his new wife to be.

Annie was shocked and confused. Her father was getting married. How could that be? It had never occurred to her that her father would want to replace her mother. She didn't want a new mother. Annie stared at this woman who she was supposed to call Mother. She wore a charcoal grey silk dress with a high collar and a white lace ruffle at the neck and poking out of the cuffs of her full length sleeves. Her hair was pulled back in a tight bun. But it was her stern, unsmiling face that caught Annie's attention.

"Hello children," said the woman. "I am sure once we get to know each other, we will all get along very well." Annie felt that her unsmiling face belied the fact that they would ever get on.

"Come children, don't be rude. Answer your mother," said Frederick.

Despite her discomfort, Annie was the first to speak. She would do anything to please her father.

"Hello Mother," she said hesitantly. All the other children then joined in, although not with great enthusiasm.

Later, when Annie and Cora escaped from the house and ran down to the river, they discussed the woman who had suddenly become their new mother.

"What do you think Annie?" said Cora, her eyes wide.

"She looks cross all the time," said Annie. "Do you think perhaps she will make father happy again?"

"I don't know about that," replied the older and wiser Cora. "I think father just wants someone to help around the house. How could he really like someone so cross looking?"

But of course, Annie and her siblings had little choice but to accept that this unknown woman had become their mother and that they must get used to having her around. Unfortunately, she had none of their own mother's gentle and caring nature. She was abrupt and set them all to do the household chores. The housekeeping had been neglected after their mother had died, but now they were all put to work to get everything back in shipshape order.

The fruit trees were bearing well. They had quinces and apples aplenty. Lillie soon had them all peeling and cutting the fruit to make quince jam and apple jelly. The delicious fruity smells filled the kitchen. The older boys set to work in the garden, pulling out weeds and generally tidying the yard. Soon the vegetable garden was again producing potatoes, turnips, tomatoes and a range of other produce.

One scorching morning in January, Annie was peering out of her window trying to spy the birds which were singing so cheerfully in the garden. She knew the familiar chortle of the magpie but could not distinguish the bird that was making the other musical sound in the old gum tree at the front of the house. As she listened carefully, she heard another sound. At first she could not work out what it was, but soon she wondered if it was a baby crying. She hurried down the stairs and joined her brothers and sisters, who were milling around her father.

"You have a new sister," their father announced with a small smile. Frederick did not smile a lot lately and Annie felt pleased. Perhaps a new baby might make her father happy again.

"Come, you may all see her now," said Frederick. "But you must be quiet."

All the children filed silently into the room where their new mother lay in bed. The baby was beside her in a tiny cradle.

Annie instantly fell in love with the pretty little baby who was peacefully sleeping with her little rosebud mouth and delicate eyelashes fluttering gently on her rosy cheeks. A tiny hand with five tiny pink fingers had escaped from the blanket she was swaddled in and Annie could not believe that any human could be so little.

Annie spent a lot of time with her new sister, who they had christened Rosa. Annie loved the name and thought it suited her new sister very well. She helped Lillie to look after her, running to fetch a nappy or heating a bottle. Sometimes she was even allowed to nurse the tiny doll-like creature.

But if Annie thought this divine little creature would be the cause of reinstating her father's happiness, she was soon disappointed. Her father still paid little heed to her or her brothers and sisters. Her prayers became more desperate. Each night as she knelt by her bed she would pray.

"Dear God, please help father to be happy."

Then she would take her rosary beads from their case and recite a decade of the rosary. When she rose after these lengthy prayer sessions, her knees were red and sore.

Then tragedy struck again.

As Annie and Cora grew up, their love of the outdoors did not diminish. Whenever they could escape from the drudgery of the housework that Lillie constantly piled upon them, they would run across the track to the river. Now that they were older, no one seemed to notice when they ventured down to the river.

Cora often bragged that she was a teenager now and that Annie ought to listen to her advice. They would sit by the banks of the river and Cora would tell Annie all about her lessons. Annie listened avidly. She worshipped the ground that Cora walked on and believed every word she said.

They sat under a gum tree, gazing out over the water. Cora opened her book and began to read.

"Cora, please read to me," said Annie. Although Annie loved to read, when she was outdoors, she struggled to sit quietly.

"You have your own book Annie," replied Cora.

"Yes, but I am sure it is not as interesting as yours."

"Well, alright then. But you must not interrupt. I want to get to the end to see what happens."

And so Cora started to read aloud. Soon Annie decided that Cora's book was not any more interesting than her own and began to fidget.

"Oh, do sit still, Annie," said Cora. "I told you I wanted to finish the book. Why don't you go for a walk whilst I read the last few pages?"

Annie was pleased to be liberated and got to her feet, put her wide-brimmed straw hat back on her head and tied the ribbons under her chin. It was cool in the shade, but it would be hot out in the sun.

Annie wandered along the riverbank for some time through the long grass, climbing over fallen branches as she went. She stopped often to inspect a pretty flower or to stare at a beetle on a tree trunk. Then Annie heard her sister call.

"Annie, where are you?"

"I am here," she called back, suddenly realising how far she had wandered. Cora's voice sounded a long way away.

She called again. "Cooee." And waited for her sister to respond. Suddenly Cora screamed. Annie jumped in fright and ran back in the direction of her sister's scream. When she reached her, Cora was sitting on the ground holding her leg.

"Snake," she said tremulously. "I have been bitten by a snake."

Annie knelt beside her sister. "What sort was it?"

"How should I know? I didn't see it for long enough. It bit me and then took off. Do something Annie, it is very painful."

Annie knew a little about snake bites. She lifted her dress and tore a strip of material from her petticoat to make a tourniquet. She could see the puncture marks on Cora's leg, just above her boot, so she tied the piece of cloth tightly around Cora's leg, above her knee.

"Can you stand up? Or should I run and get help?'

"I think I can stand."

Annie helped Cora to her feet and looped Cora's arm over her shoulder. The two girls began to limp back to the house. But they had a good distance to cover and soon Cora was leaning heavily on Annie. Annie looked on in horror as Cora vomited.

"I can't see properly. Everything is fuzzy."

"I don't think you should try to walk any further. Sit down here and I will run home to get help. It is not far now," Annie said with a confidence that she did not feel.

Annie left her sister sitting with her back against a large rock and ran as fast as she could. Annie burst into the kitchen.

"Help! A snake has bitten Cora."

Fortunately, her older brother, Howard, was sitting at the table drinking a cup of tea with Lillie. Howard was a tall, strong young man. Despite the fact that he was only fifteen, he had been helping out in the family's butchery for several years.

"What?" he exclaimed. "Where is she?"

"Down by the river. Hurry, we must get to her. She looks terrible."

Annie ran out the door, closely followed by Howard and Lillie. They ran at full pelt until they reached the spot where Cora sat, her breathing becoming laboured. Without wasting a second, Howard picked Cora up and ran back towards the house.

"We must get a doctor," said Howard. "Annie, go into town and see if you can find Dr Nicholson."

"But I want to stay with Cora."

"Don't argue, Annie," said Lillie. "Go."

Annie did not put up any further protest but went running off to the ford to cross the river into the town. She continued running up the lane way into the main street and knocked at the Doctor's door.

"Oh thank goodness," she cried as the Doctor opened the door. "You must hurry. Cora has been bitten by a snake."

The Doctor did not waste any time. He grabbed his bag and followed Annie back across the ford to the house. Cora was lying on the chaise lounge in the drawing room. By now, Cora was weak and could barely move.

The doctor opened his bag and laid out his instruments. He took a scalpel and made an incision across the puncture mark, hoping that the bleeding would remove some of the poison. Annie and her family looked on, horrified, as the blood started to flow.

Cora screamed as the Doctor then poured ammonia over the wound. Annie cringed and tears ran down her face as she cried silently. Finally, he took a bottle of brandy and poured a generous amount into a glass. Although Cora was barely conscious by now, he managed to pour a liberal amount down her throat.

"Is she going to be alright Doctor?" asked Lillie. Annie held her breath as the Doctor answered.

"I really have no way of knowing. The paralysis seems to be starting. There is little that I can do for her now. We must wait and see."

"It is all my fault," sobbed Annie. "If I had not wandered off so far, she would not have had to follow me. We were so far from home. Maybe if we had gotten here quicker..." Her voice trailed off. No one disagreed with her, which made her feel all the worse.

The Doctor, knowing there was little else he could do for now, packed up his bag and left the family to their worrying.

"Howard, go to the shop and fetch your father," said Lillie.

Annie looked at Howard beseechingly.

"Yes, please hurry," she said. "Father will know what to do."

Howard looked at Lillie, doubting that there was anything his father could do, but he left the house quickly.

Footsteps echoed down the hall as Howard returned with Frederick. He looked at his daughter, his face white with dread. By now Cora was lying quietly moaning but unable to move, her breathing shallow and laboured. Indeed, she appeared to be losing consciousness and slipping away from them. Lillie waved smelling salts under her nose, which caused her eyes to flicker but did not revive her.

The Doctor returned later in the day to check on her.

"I am sorry, but I don't think she is going to pull through," he announced sadly.

Annie let out a gut-wrenching cry.

"Doctor, please. Surely there is something more you can do?" she cried.

The Doctor turned to Frederick with a look of concern.

"There is one more thing I can try. There are some doctors who have been using injections of strychnine to treat snake bite with some success."

When Frederick nodded, the Doctor took a large syringe from his bag and injected Cora with a dose of strychnine.

"Now all we can do is wait," he said. "But you must not get your hopes up. She is very ill."

The family kept a silent vigil as Cora slipped into a coma. She died quietly in the early morning without waking. Annie was heartbroken. She sat and held her sister, crying bitter tears, until her father pulled her away.

The funeral was held three days later, on a day when the sun shone brightly. Annie felt it would have been more fitting if it had been a dull, cloudy day. Annie and her family were all, once again, dressed in black mourning clothes as they stood at the graveside to hear Father Daly say prayers over Cora's coffin. Her father had made the small timber coffin for his daughter.

As the coffin was lowered into the grave, a cloud passed over the sun. Annie felt that was as it should be. The sun would never shine on her special sister again.

Annie leaned in close to her father as they stood beside the grave, but he moved away. She was sure that he blamed her for this second awful tragedy in his life.

Chapter Ten

Autumn was upon them. This was usually Annie's favourite time of the year. She watched as the leaves on the trees in the garden turned to bright reds, yellows and oranges. The only drawback was that autumn heralded the winter, which was Annie's least favourite season. Every year, as the days grew shorter and the skies greyer, Annie felt the melancholy fall on her. This year being locked away intensified the feelings of loss of control and sadness. There still seemed no prospect of Annie being able to gain her freedom. There was no word from her father. It seemed impossible that he would simply leave her to her fate without so much as a word.

By now she was getting to know some of the women in the ward and was rather surprised that many of them were just like her. From what she had heard of mental asylums before her admission, she imagined wild scenes with women screaming and banging their heads against the walls. But many of them did not appear to be mad at all, once she got to know them. They came from all walks of life. Many had been forced onto the streets by the depression which was biting hard in Victoria. The women related their stories of having to try to keep a roof over their heads and look after the children when their husbands had gone off to find work. Many had found themselves evicted from their homes with no means of support. Vagrancy laws were such that they ended up in the asylum.

Helena was a great source of comfort to Annie and they became fast friends. Together they discussed the other women. Helena told Annie which women to beware of and which were quite sane and could be relied upon for support.

Catherine was one person who Annie was very curious about. Annie had spoken to her on several occasions and she had seemed completely sensible and normal.

"Why is she here?" asked Annie.

"She has been here for many years," replied Helena. "I feel very sorry for her. As you have noticed, she is quite sensible and really should not be here. I am thankful that she has her embroidery to keep her busy, otherwise she might actually go insane."

"So why hasn't she been released?"

"Apparently her family does not want her to be released. When she came here she was diagnosed with puerperal insanity, so the Doctors told her, after the birth of her sixth child. She had become highly emotional and delusional. She believed she had not given birth to her child at all. Her husband had her committed because he thought she could not be cured and he did not want a sick wife looking after his children. Apparently, he now has a live-in nanny who looks after the children." Helena gave Annie a wink.

But Annie was a naïve country girl with little understanding of childbirth and the philandering ways of some men.

"What do you mean?"

"Well, I don't think the nanny is just in the house for the sake of the children."

"I still don't understand."

"Catherine suspects he is having an affair with the nanny."

"What? You mean he is being unfaithful to his wife?"

"Well, that is what Catherine believes. And I must say, I would not be surprised. I can't imagine a man having a pretty young thing in his household and, believing that he has gotten rid of his wife, not being tempted to seduce her."

Annie was astonished. She had never come across any man who had been unfaithful to his wife. Her father's work was his whole life. She could not imagine him straying to another woman, even though her stepmother had become quite bitter and hard to live with since the family had moved to Timor. She thought of her older sister, who seemed happy with her lot as a married woman. But she wondered if she would even know if her husband was having an affair.

"But what is it you said she was suffering from? Puerperal insanity? What is that?" she asked. Annie certainly felt she was getting an education today. Her stepmother had not really explained much about relationships with men. She had to rely on getting what information she could from her sister, who was unfortunately not very forthcoming.

"I am not completely sure. But I know that women who suffer from it seem quite insane for a time. But many recover, as Catherine has."

"I don't wonder that you feel sorry for her. I wish there was something we could do to help her."

"Be careful, Annie," said Helena. "The staff don't take kindly to inmates interfering."

Annie eventually lost faith that her father would ever come for her. With little else to do each day, there was plenty of time to think. Slowly Annie's troubled thoughts became clearer. She came to the realisation that there was nothing she could do to get out of the asylum, apart from controlling her emotions to convince the medical staff she did not need to be here. She decided that the best course of action would be to try to make the most of her fate for the time being and to behave like a model inmate. It was frustrating and difficult, but somehow she must make a life within these walls until something changed.

Each day was the same as the last. So far, Annie had found very little to relieve the boredom. She liked to read, but there were only a few books and it was hard to find any peace in the rowdy surroundings where she could read without distractions. She knew that if the women were willing to work, they could be employed in the garden or the laundry. Or she could also have worked in the sewing room where they made all the women's garments, but she was not an accomplished seamstress. No one had been interested in teaching her this skill after the death of her mother. Her stepmother had tried but had soon become impatient with Annie's lack of aptitude for needlework and gave up.

Up until now, Annie had avoided work apart from the daily chores that all the women performed. It had taken some time for her to become accustomed to being incarcerated and that, in all likelihood, no one was coming to rescue her. But now she decided to ask the attendants if she could work in the garden with Helena. Annie had always enjoyed working in the garden, planting and tending the vegetables at home.

The attendants were only too pleased to put Annie to work. There was plenty of work to be done after all. There were not enough attendants, and it seemed that some of them were lazy and dodged the dirty jobs like cleaning up after incontinent inmates. Often attendants called on the inmates to remove the soiled straw mattresses from the beds and take them to the barns where the covers were cleaned and filled with fresh straw.

"You can work in the garden, but that is a privilege," said the attendant. "We only allow inmates to work in the garden if they agree to take their turn in the laundry."

Annie was not afraid of hard work so soon she was working in the laundry, washing the linen and the inmates' clothing in the huge coppers, dunking the washing with a long stout stick, and scrubbing it on the duckboards. Her arms, bare to the elbows, soon became reddened and dry. Two women would work together to wring out the sheets and larger items between them and hang them on the lines. It was hot and heavy work. The smell of bleach and rough soap filled the air. But at least it filled in the time.

After a few days, Annie had earned the right to work in the garden. This was the only time that Annie felt any peace at all. Her nostrils would be filled with the pleasant scent of the flowers and the stronger smells of rosemary and thyme in the herb garden. When the wind was in the right direction and when the women working around her were quiet, she fancied she could even hear the sound of the water rushing down the nearby Yarra river. Despite the harshness of her situation, Annie felt almost at peace getting her hands dirty in the garden.

But as the weeks passed, she grew more anxious. She wondered if she would ever be allowed to leave this place.

One of the few things that helped Annie to survive the horror of her early days in the asylum, apart from her work in the garden, were the Sunday church services. The services were held in the dining hall and were attended by both male and female inmates. This was the only time that Annie and the other women saw the male inmates. The men were housed separately in the east wing of the asylum. But even though they attended the services together, the men and women were still not allowed to fraternise. The two groups sat separately on long forms, moved into place for the services, men on the right side and women on the left. Annie had heard that some women had been committed because they were considered to be unable to control their sexual desires, so the attendants kept a very close eye on them when the men were around.

There were two services each Sunday. Those of the Roman Catholic faith attended a morning service whilst all the other religions were grouped as protestants and attended their service in the afternoon.

Attending a church service was only allowed for those inmates who were well behaved. So there were usually around 30 women at most of the services.

Annie was pleased to be able to attend Mass as she still felt comforted by her religious beliefs. Her mind felt clear as the priest spoke the familiar Latin words of the mass in a singsong voice. He was not the regular fire and brimstone priest like Father Daly. This priest's sermons were mundane and comforting. Annie wondered if he had given up hope of saving any of the lunatics in his congregation. The sound of his voice was soothing. The warm smell of the candles and the spicy incense calmed her.

She would never forsake her religion altogether. She still felt a special closeness to her mother when she attended Mass. In the depths of his grief, her father had refused to allow her to attend Mass for several years after her mother's death. She now felt certain that this had contributed to her obsession to pursue her faith at all costs.

Elsie had just returned to her office after doing the rounds of the dormitories with Doctor Woodforde. As usual after these inspections she felt more than a little annoyed. The Doctor never took more than a minute to really assess the situation that the women were having to contend with. Although she made every effort to ensure conditions were as good as they could be, with the limited resources available to her, she felt that many of the women needed more careful treatment, whilst still others really should be assessed for release. But the more she tried to convince the doctor of her opinions, the less he seemed to listen to her.

There was a knock at her office door. One of the attendants entered saying that there was a visitor for Annie.

"Who is it?"

"It is a priest, he says his name is Father Daly."

Elsie frowned. She was disappointed that it was not Annie's father or at least some member of her family. She thought carefully. She wondered if it would be a good idea for Annie to have a visit from a priest given that the cause of her problems had been attributed to religious mania. Annie had certainly seemed very confused about the place of religion in her life when she had been admitted. She had only been with them for a few weeks, not a long time by usual standards. Elsie felt that Annie was finally settling in and perhaps beginning to recover. A visit like this might set her back.

"Show him in," she said to the attendant.

Father Daly was a big man, standing over six feet. He had a stern face with dark eyes and bushy eyebrows; a rather imposing figure. He was dressed in black except for his white collar.

"Please take a seat father," said Elsie. "How can I help you?"

"I am here to see Annie Moore," he responded, his voice low and gruff.

"I am very sorry but we do not allow the inmates to have visitors so early in their treatment."

"That would hardly apply to me, Matron. I am Annie's spiritual teacher. You are probably not aware that she was to become a nun."

"I was not aware of that but it makes no difference. Perhaps you could return in another month or so when Annie is more settled. I am sure she will be pleased to see you then."

She rose from her seat indicating that the interview was over and walked with Father Daly to the entrance.

"Thank you father, and goodbye."

Father Daly was obviously not pleased but did not argue further.

Later that day Elsie was called to see Annie. She was curled up on the floor in a corner of the dayroom in obvious distress. An attendant was standing beside her.

"What is going on here?" asked the matron.

"She has just had a visit with her priest," replied the attendant. "She seemed pleased to hear that he had come to see her but when she returned from the visit she was screaming and hitting out at the other inmates. I was about to restrain her when she suddenly went quiet and slumped into the chair. She has not moved since. Should I call the Doctor?"

"No, that will be all thank you. I will talk to her now."

Elsie talked gently to Annie but there was no response. Her anger was bubbling underneath. Who had allowed this visit?

"Helena, will you please sit with Annie and try to keep her calm. I need to speak to the Doctor."

"Of course Matron," replied Helena. "I will watch her. I am sure she will come out of it soon."

Elsie got up and hurried to Doctor Woodforde's office. She knocked loudly on the door. The Doctor called for her to enter.

"Doctor Woodforde, did you allow Father Daly to visit Annie Moore."

"Well good morning, Matron. Yes, I did, as if it is any of your business."

"But surely you are aware of how that might have effected Annie so early in her treatment?"

Doctor Woodford's eyes narrowed and his brow was furrowed.

"I beg your pardon, Matron Lansdowne. Are you trying to tell me how to treat my patients?"

Elsie drew a deep breath and tried to calm her anger. She knew from experience that in order to make any impression on the Doctor, she needed to stay calm.

"Of course not Doctor, but I had already told Father Daly that it was too early for Annie to have visitors."

"Well, I don't agree, Matron. That will be all thank you."

Elsie hurried back to her office so that no one would see how angry she was. She paced up and down wondering how she was supposed to help these women without any authority.

Helena sat with Annie for some time before Annie began to come out of her trancelike state.

"Annie, are you alright? It's me, Helena." Annie turned her head to look at Helena but her eyes were still blank.

"Please, Annie. Say something. What has happened?"

All of a sudden Annie started to sob, her shoulders shaking violently. Helena reached out and held her gently until the sobs subsided.

"Tell me what happened Annie," Helena asked again as gently as she could.

"It's Father Daly," said Annie through her tears. Her voice was choked and she took deep gasps of breath.

"He is so angry with me." Again she was overtaken by deep wracking sobs. "I should never have left. God will never forgive me. I am going to hell, I know it."

"Oh Annie, that is simply not true. You are a good person," said Helena but this only made Annie sob harder. Helena sat with Annie, huddled in the corner for several hours before Annie calmed down.

"I am more confused than ever Helena," said Annie. "It is so troubling that Father Daly is angry with me. He said I have sinned greatly by running away. He said that my father had told him where he might find me. Helena, can you believe my father has known I am locked up in here all this time and has not come to see me? But Father Daly would not give me any news of my family. He just went on and on about my becoming a nun when I get out of here. What am I to do?"

"Annie, I can see your religion is important to you, but you need time to recover from this confusion. Give yourself time. I am sure your God will forgive you. Father Daly is only a man after all. Perhaps you would be better to pray for guidance rather than placing so much store on what Father Daly says."

Chapter Eleven

Annie moved quickly around the large well-equipped kitchen in their Avoca home as she prepared the evening meal. It was a warm summer evening, and the windows were open, letting in a welcome fresh breeze. The last of the sun's rays shone into the kitchen and highlighted the dust that moved through the air, making it dance.

It was four years since Cora had died and Annie still felt her loss with every fibre of her being. There was no one she could really confide in anymore. Her father was still as cold with her as he had been since her mother had died. And she still believed that he blamed her for Cora's death. Her older brothers and sisters had left home to make their own way. Annie dreamed of one day being able to marry and have a house and family of her own. But she had to bury her dreams. As the youngest of Ellen's children, she was the only one left at home and had no alternative other than to make herself useful by looking after the younger children. She could not even escape by going to school anymore. When she had turned twelve, her father deemed she had enough education and must stay home to help her stepmother. She had few things in her life that made her happy. She loved to read and to walk by the river. But as each year passed, there was more work for her to do and she had less time for these favourite activities. Her stepmother had borne three more children after Rosa, so the house was once again full of the constant noise of four young children. Annie could, however, still seek solace in her music. She played the piano and sang, which the younger children enjoyed, so at least her stepmother encouraged this activity. But she was desperately unhappy.

After her mother died, her father had declared that they would not be attending mass anymore, and she had missed the ritual of going to church on Sundays. Her older siblings did not really seem to mind, but Annie had felt the loss sorely as time wore on. She was a teenager now. Surely, she could make up her own mind about attending mass?

The first time she had made up her mind to return to her religion, it had caused another argument with her stepmother.

"I would like to go to mass this morning," she announced.

"Oh would you just, and who is going to prepare the vegetables for the roast?" said Lillie.

Her father was seated in an easy chair by the stove in the kitchen reading a newspaper. He said nothing.

"I can do them when I get back."

"So I suppose you expect us to wait until who knows when for our meal, just so that you can go to church?"

Annie put her teacup down on the table rather too roughly.

"Well, you could do them yourself."

Her father looked up from his paper.

"That is enough, young lady. That is no way to talk to your mother. You will apologise."

But by now, Annie was too angry to apologise. She went into the bedroom to put on her good straw hat and gloves and collected her prayer book before storming out of the house.

Annie walked towards the river and over the bridge. As she walked, she felt her temper begin to cool and a calmness wash over her. As the church spire came into view, she knew that this was what had been missing in her life. She felt that all her problems could be solved if she just renewed her faith.

She entered the church through the huge timber doors and from the porch she could see that there were a good number of people in attendance. Suddenly she felt out of place, as it had been such a long time since she had last been to Mass. She knew that missing Sunday Mass was a sin. She put her head down and slipped into an empty pew at the rear of the church. Throughout the service, she kept her eyes lowered and her head bowed so that her hat partially covered her face.

The organ started to play and the voices of the congregation combined to sing *How Great Thou Art* as Father Daly strode onto the altar. As the song soared to its conclusion, he recited the opening prayers and then everyone took their seats for the sermon. It did not surprise Annie to hear the priest launch into a tirade of hellfire and brimstone and how, if they did not repent their sins, the congregation would face eternal damnation. But somehow she was comforted as she was transported back in time, snuggling into her mother in order to feel secure against the loud, angry voice of the priest.

Annie had made her first confession and communion at school but had not kept up the sacraments, so she could not go to communion until she had confessed all her sins. As the Mass concluded, and the congregation filed out of the church, Annie sat, keeping her head lowered, hoping that Father Daly would enter the confessional so that she might cleanse her soul by confessing.

Eventually, Father Daly came down the aisle and went into the confessional. Annie was pleased to see that there were very few people lining up for confession this morning, so she did not have to wait long until it was her turn.

She opened the door, next to the one where the priest had entered, and knelt down. She felt the familiar anxiety that confessing her sins had always caused. The priest slid back the panel. She could only see the outline of his head behind the screen. Although she knew that the priest was not allowed to tell anyone about her sins, she still felt shy and anxious about what she was about to say.

"Bless me father, for I have sinned," Annie managed to stammer the words required to begin her confession.

"What are your sins?" asked the priest.

Annie paused for a moment and then launched into the long list of sins that she had prepared.

"I told lies and was rude to my stepmother. I went down to the river when I wasn't supposed to." Then she paused again as she got ready to relate what she considered to be her worst sin. "I am jealous of my half-sister and brothers because they get more attention from my father. And I don't like my stepmother." Annie held her breath, waiting for the priest to say something.

"That is a long list of sins, young lady," said the priest. "You must repent and try harder to be kind to your family. For penance, you must say two decades of the rosary." Then the shadowy figure of the priest made a sign of the cross and the panel slid back into place. She knew she could now escape from the confessional.

She slid back into the pew and said a few quiet prayers before she left the church, feeling relieved that God had now forgiven her sins and she could go to communion next Sunday. She felt light as she made her way home, feeling that a weight had been lifted off her now that she was, for the moment, free of sin. But soon she knew she must face her stepmother again, and she wondered if she would be able to keep her temper in check.

It was not long before her resolve was tested. When she arrived home she barely had time to take off her hat, and put it away along with her gloves and prayerbook, before her stepmother was berating her for taking so long and not getting the vegetables on for the Sunday roast. She would really have liked to have done her penance, but she knew that would have to wait. She quickly got the vegetables into the oven. Soon they were sizzling in the pan with the leg of lamb. The smell of roasting meat and vegetables filled the room and Annie felt pangs of hunger gnawing at her stomach. No wonder the children were becoming fractious if they were as hungry as she was.

"Annie, for goodness sake, take the children outside," said Lillie. "They need to run around for a bit while the dinner cooks. If you had been here we could have been eating by now."

Annie ignored her stepmother's jibe and called to the children. "Come on, let's go play for a while."

"But I am hungry," said Rosa.

"I know," said Annie. "Be patient. Dinner won't be too much longer."

The boys found the cricket bat and ball and they had a spirited game of cricket with the boys doing the batting and bowling whilst Annie and Rosa had to be content with the fielding.

Annie was glad to be called back inside to dish up the dinner. By now everyone was ravenous, so once everyone had been served, a blessed silence descended as the family ate their Sunday roast. Then Annie was called on to clear the table and wash the dishes. Only after all that was done was she able to escape the house with her favourite book and find a shady spot down by the river for a few minutes of peace.

That evening, she knelt beside her bed to say her penance. She recited all five decades of the rosary, just to be on the safe side.

As the months wore on and she became more engrossed in the doctrines of the church, she began to wonder if she was being called by God. Last week Father Daly had preached about vocations in his sermon. He had said that the congregation had a responsibility to dedicate their lives to God. He talked about those who took vows and became priests and nuns. Was this what she was destined for? Lately she had felt that she needed to do something to pay for her constant sinning. She found it so hard to be kind and considerate to her stepmother. Maybe God was calling her to become a nun? But despite her wish to make up for her sins, she tried to put it from her mind. She did not want to become a nun. She wanted to find a kind man to marry and have a family of her own.

Annie's prayer sessions each night became longer as she prayed for guidance and for forgiveness for her sins. Each time she made her vow to God that she would be better. But the next day would come, and she would be unable to keep her promises and she would repeat the previous day's sins. This played heavily on her mind. Sometimes she felt she must be going mad. How could she expect anything good to happen to her when she was a sinner? Although she was now regularly attending confession, she did not seem to be able to control her jealousy and her unkind feelings for her stepmother. But the turmoil within her mind just became worse the more she prayed about it.

Annie continued to attend Mass and confession as she grew up despite the extra troubles it caused with her stepmother. By the time she was seventeen years old she was certain she was going to hell. She committed the same sins over and over. Her anguish at not having any time to herself and not being able to attend any of the social events that other young girls of her acquaintance were attending continued to grow. She was a young woman now. Surely, she should have a social life? How would she ever meet a wonderful man and fall in love? Her older sister, Bertha, had only been a couple of years older than Annie was now when she had married. It was all so unfair. Each time she went to confession, the priest berated her, telling her she would face eternal damnation if she did not make peace with her stepmother. Her penance grew more each time.

But now things were going from bad to worse. Her father had been talking about the butcher shop not doing as well as he hoped. He said there was a depression, and people could not afford to buy meat.

Annie and Lillie were preparing the evening meal and, as usual, the children were complaining about being hungry when Frederick came home one evening with an announcement. He gave Lillie a despairing look.

"I have to take a job at the mines. We can't hold out any longer."

"What do you mean, Frederick?" asked Lillie.

"They are looking for a mine carpenter at the Grand Duke mine in Timor. I have accepted the job because we can't keep going on like this with no money coming in."

"How could you have done that without talking to me first?"

"Lillie, please, not in front of the children."

"I am sorry, Frederick, but I won't be put off. How can you work in Timor?"

"We will have to move. I have found a place for us to rent."

"That is ridiculous, Frederick. We can't just up and move on a whim."

"I am not doing this on a whim, Lillie. We have no choice. The butchery is not bringing in the income we need. It won't be forever. Just until we get back on our feet again. This depression can't last forever. Once people can afford to buy meat again, I will reopen the butcher shop."

"But what about the tenants?" said Lillie. "Surely that must be helping?" Frederick owned several properties in the street, which were rented out to miners in the area.

"Lillie, surely you are not so blind as to be able to see that they are struggling too. Many of them have been laid off from the mine and have not paid their rent for weeks. We cannot rely on that income. We are just lucky that I have skills as a carpenter otherwise I might not have work either."

Annie listened to this conversation, as she prepared the evening meal, feeling the panic rising in her chest. What would this mean? Timor was a tiny town with not much to offer. She wondered what she would do if she couldn't go to confession and talk to Father Daly. She didn't even know if there was a catholic church at Timor.

"Father, must we go?" she asked. Her father gave her a withering look and she lowered her eyes but could not help but continue. "I could get work."

"Don't be foolish," said Lillie. "I need your help in the house."

"That's enough," said Frederick. "There will be no more discussion. I have made my decision and there is nothing more to be said."

The family sat down to a very tense meal as Frederick related his plans.

And so the family moved to Timor. The furniture in the house in Avoca was covered with sheets and the house was locked up. As they were not expecting to be gone for long they took only the bare essentials with them. Annie was horrified when she saw the small cottage that the whole family were to live in and she knew Lillie would not be happy and that her ill temper and her demands on Annie's time would be sure to grow.

"Frederick, surely you don't expect us to live here?" Lillie moaned. "Where will we all sleep?"

"Please Lillie, we must make do. When will you understand that we don't have a choice?"

Chapter Twelve

Annie sat listlessly on her bed. When would this nightmare end? She was more and more convinced that she was not meant to be locked up in this place. As she looked around her, at the other women who shared this large dormitory with her, she knew that many of them should not be there either. She had heard many stories of her fellow inmates being incarcerated by husbands or fathers who had simply wanted to get rid of the women.

Suddenly a scream rang out from the other end of the dormitory. Annie sat up and saw that one of the women was lying on the floor convulsing.

"Help, someone please help," came a shout from the girl in the bed next to the poor, unfortunate woman. Soon two attendants were on the scene. Annie was not pleased to see that one of them was Sheila. She had taken quite a dislike to the bad-tempered attendant.

"Leave her be," Sheila said. "There is nothing we can do but wait for the episode to be over." With that, she roughly dragged the woman away from the bed and any other objects upon which she could hurt herself. The fit went on for some minutes.

The woman's body arched and her head was thrown backwards with the convulsions. The whites of her eyes showed as they rolled back in her head. Annie was horrified. This was the first time she had seen such a fit, although she had heard others talk of them. As the convulsions slowed, the woman started to come to her senses and the attendants finally took some action to assist.

"Help me get her onto the bed," said Sheila.

Together with two of the women, they half lifted, half dragged the hapless woman onto her bed.

"What happened?" asked the woman, as she blinked her eyes.

"You had another fit," said the second attendant. "You will be all right. You just need to rest. The doctor will check on you when he does his rounds tomorrow."

The fit had obviously taken its toll on the woman and she soon fell into a fitful sleep.

Annie was worried for her.

"Shouldn't we get the doctor immediately?" she asked the attendant.

"Oh, there is no need for that," replied Sheila. "These fits happen all the time with the epileptics. The Doctor will see her tomorrow."

"But surely someone should see her now? You can see that she looks awful. She is so pale."

"You are Annie, aren't you?" asked Sheila.

"Yes, that's right, can't you see that this woman needs to be cared for properly."

"So Annie, you think you know better than me? Is that the case? Let me remind you who is in charge here. You would do well to mind your own business and not get in my way."

Annie frowned at Sheila but decided there was little more she could do to convince her that a Doctor should be called. Instead she sat in the chair by the woman's bed stroking her hand, hoping that her presence would provide some comfort to the poor woman.

Helena also came and sat with the woman. Annie could not help feeling angry at the treatment of the epileptic woman.

"That attendant is very mean, the one I think is called Sheila," she said to Helena.

"Her name is Sheila Murphy," said Helena. "And you would do well to keep out of her way. She can be very cruel."

"Did you see how she treated this poor woman? She had no sympathy for her."

"I know but that is her way. She has worked here for a long time and can be rather impatient. But really Annie, for your own sake, you should not get in her way. You need to choose your battles and know that there are very few that you can win in here."

"But it is so cruel, just to leave her there."

"I know it seems that way, but you must realise there is actually very little that can be done when someone has a fit. At least Sheila moved her away from anything that she could hurt herself on as she thrashed about."

Annie looked at the poor woman, who was still murmuring and tossing in her sleep. She continued to hold her hand, hoping to soothe the woman.

Annie had been in the asylum for several months before she heard anything from home. She was still angry and upset that she had not heard from her father especially as Father Daly had told her that her family knew where she was. The midday meal that day seemed worse than usual. Not that it was really any different. There was very little variety in their daily meals other than bread and butter and grisly meat.

Suddenly there was a letter dropped on the table beside her plate. She looked up at the attendant who had brought the letter.

"Well, go on, open it," said the attendant amused at Annie's confusion.

"What is it?" asked Annie.

"What do you think it is?" asked the attendant. "Have you never seen a letter before?"

"I have never had a letter in here."

"Yes, and you are not likely to get many more. You are very lucky that the matron allowed you to have this one."

Her hands shook as she picked up the letter. The address was written in a child's hand. It was from Rosa. Before she even opened the letter, she felt her anger rise again knowing her father could have come for her. For all she knew he hadn't even enquired to see if she was alive and well. She thought of Rosa. It was not her fault, and it was a blessing to see her sister's writing. Slowly she opened the letter and unfolded the single sheet of paper and began to read.

Dear Annie

I hope you are well. I miss you very much. You have been gone for such a long time. I asked father where you were and at first he said he did not know. He said he would try to find you and now that he has he said that it would be alright if I wrote to you.

Everyone is well here, but we need you to come home. The boys are fighting all the time and mother gets very cross with us. When will you be able to come, Annie?

I hope this letter finds you well.

Your loving sister

Rosa

Tears welled in Annie's eyes as she folded the letter and returned it to the envelope. It was bittersweet to receive the letter, knowing that Rosa missed her and wanted her to come home. But she was disturbed by the knowledge that her father had told Rosa that he didn't know where she was. Annie had been told that both the police and Matron Lansdowne had tried to contact him when she was first arrested.

It surprised Annie that they had passed the letter on to her. Very few people received letters there and when Annie enquired, they had told her that most of the letters were censored and only those that were considered appropriate were given to the women. Often, they would just be summoned to the matron's office and told of the partial contents of letters from home. But they were not allowed to read them. Annie considered herself very fortunate that she had been given the letter from Rosa and tucked it carefully away in her pocket. She wondered where she would keep this treasured possession. Their belongings, including their clothing, all had to be left in the dayroom. How could she be sure that her letter would not be lost or destroyed? Perhaps if she kept it in her pocket, she could smuggle it into her bag, which was still stored under her bed, with her bible and rosary beads.

She wanted more than anything to write back to Rosa. It distressed her that the girl would not really understand why Annie had left them. So she sought out one of the kinder attendants and asked for paper and pen.

When the writing tools arrived, she took them with her into the yard so that she could find a quiet place to write where no one would disturb her.

Dear Rosa

I hope this letter finds you well and that you are looking after your brothers and sister. I miss you very much too, so it was wonderful to get your letter. I am really sorry that I had to leave, but as you know, I was sad and needed to get away to sort out my thoughts.

It is not so bad here, Rosa. I have made some wonderful friends. We are well fed, and I am allowed to work in the garden. You know how much I love getting my hands dirty to make the flowers and vegetables grow.

So please don't worry about me. I am doing well. Tell father I am well and that I would love to hear from him. I hope I can see you very soon.

Your loving sister
Annie.

As Annie got to know more of the women, she was astonished to find out that many of them wanted to be there. Their lives on the outside had been horrendous. Even worse than being locked up in there, if that was possible.

"The last thing I want is to get out of here," said the young girl next to her as they sat at the long deal table eating their meal. Annie had been attracted to her because she seemed quite happy and content most of the time. Helena had told her that the girl's name was Mabel Johnson. She looked very young, possibly even younger than Annie, but Annie thought she seemed wise to the ways of the world.

"What do you mean?" asked Annie, looking at the girl with astonishment. She was very pretty, with fine curly hair framing her pixie-like face when she wasn't trying to tame it in long plaits. She looked at Annie with huge, dark eyes.

"I have everything I need in here. Three meals a day, a roof over my head and a comfy bed to sleep in. Why would I want to be anywhere else? There is nothing for me on the outside."

"Don't you have any family?"

"My parents both died when I was very young and my older sister looked after us as best she could. But eventually we could not pay the rent and they turned us out onto the street."

"So you didn't you have anywhere to live? How did you survive?"

Mabel looked at Annie and smiled sadly.

"We all tried to stay together and look after each other for a while. But eventually we went our separate ways. My brothers were able to get enough odd jobs to be able to survive, but it was harder for my sister and me. My sister was fortunate and found work cleaning in a hotel. But I was not so lucky. I eventually had no choice and did what I had to do. I met a man who said he would look out for me, but I soon found out that all he cared about was taking his cut of the money."

"Money? What money?"

"You really don't understand, do you? You must have led a very sheltered life. I had to provide favors for men. It was the only way I had to survive."

Annie was shocked. "Do you mean you slept with men and they paid you?"

"Yes, Annie, it is not so unusual you know. There are many women on the streets or in brothels who have no other way to support themselves. It is a hard life, particularly if you don't have anyone looking out for you. It was bad enough having to sleep with the men, but the cruel ones would beat me as well. It was not the way anyone would want to live. And most of the time I feared for my life. Which is why it was the best day of my life when the police found me and brought me here."

"I can't believe it," said Annie. "That they would lock you away when it was others that were hurting you."

"That is the way it is for women with no prospects. It is a tough world out there. So many are out of work and have nowhere to live and have to beg for food."

"Now I can understand why you are happy to stay here. But what will you do if they decide you are well enough to be released?"

"That's not likely to happen because I will just put on an act, throw a fit or two. But if they did decide to release me, that would be the end. I would find a way to end my life. I simply cannot return to the streets."

"Surely not? There must be another way."

"Yes, there is, and that is to make sure I can stay here."

Annie felt very fortunate to be able to work in the garden and the laundry. It filled the days and gave her something to think about other than the misery of being locked away. She of course enjoyed her work in the garden with Helena the most. It was harder working outside now that the winter was approaching and it was becoming colder. Annie knew that eventually the garden would come back to life as the seasons moved on but hopefully she would not be here by then.

The laundry work was much more demanding but despite the difficult conditions and the hard work, she and Mabel became very close working in there together.

For six hours a day, they worked in the hot, steamy laundry. The only respite from the heat was when they went outside to hang the washing on the lines. Hundreds of sheets billowed in the wind on these cold winter days.

As they hung the washing, Sheila Murphy appeared behind them. Annie ignored her and continued to hang the washing.

Sheila glared at Mabel. "Not like that, you lazy girl. You must pull the sheets taught."

In her anxiety at being berated, Mabel dropped the pillow cases she was holding, and they landed in the dust at her feet.

"Now look what you have done." Sheila grabbed Mabel's hair, which hung down her back in plaits, and dragged her face towards the dirt. "Pick them up. Now they will have to be washed all over again."

Mabel tried to pull away, but that only made Sheila angry.

"Don't you fight against me or I will have to restrain you."

Mabel continued to struggle, but Sheila then grabbed her around the neck from behind, immobilising her in a headlock.

Annie was horrified. She could see that Mabel was struggling to breathe. This was not the first time she had seen Sheila being rough with the women.

"Stop it, you are hurting her."

Sheila turned on her with eyes glowing with hatred. "What did you say?"

"I asked you to stop. If you don't let her go, I will report you to Matron Lansdowne."

By now Sheila's face was purple with rage. She let go of Mabel and turned on Annie.

"How dare you, you stupid girl! As if Matron Lansdowne will listen to anything you have to say. Get back to your work." With that, Sheila turned on her heels left the two girls standing there looking nervously at each other.

"Are you alright?" Annie asked the frightened Mabel, who was looking pale and scared.

"I will be. I just need to get my breath back. It was nice of you to stand up for me, Annie. But it is not a good idea to make enemies of the attendants. And that one is particularly mean."

"I know. Helena has already warned me about her, but I can't just stand by and say nothing when people are being treated so appallingly."

"I think you may have scared her off when you mentioned Matron Lansdowne. Do you really think the matron would listen to your complaint?"

"I don't really know, but we will soon find out. I am definitely going to talk to her."

"I don't know Annie. I am not sure that is a good idea?"

"Oh I am certain it won't do any harm. Matron Lansdowne seems to be a kind woman beneath her gruff exterior. She has been kind to me at least."

Mabel picked up the pillowcases and took them back to be laundered again. Then the two young women picked up the next sheet and each took hold of an end and began twisting it to wring out the water.

Annie had eventually decided not to report Sheila to the matron after talking to Helena.

"Annie you must reconsider," advised Helena. "Do you really want to make an enemy of Sheila?"

"So you think I should just let her get away with it?" said Annie indignantly.

"Actually, yes, that is exactly what I think. You mustn't get offside with Sheila. Don't forget that you need to appear to be calm and a model inmate if you ever want to leave this place."

So Annie had taken the advice of her older friend and had not reported Sheila.

But it was not long before Annie realised it was rather too late, and that she had already made an enemy of Sheila Murphy. Any chance she got, Sheila would berate and harass her. She would continually find fault with everything that Annie did. Annie became angry and lost patience with this constant harassment. She decided she had to do something.

She asked one of the attendants if she could speak to Matron Lansdowne.

"Well, I don't think it is likely that she will have time for a private audience," said the attendant, the sarcasm evident in her voice.

"Can you please ask her?" said Annie, trying to be patient.

The attendant walked away without answering Annie, but sometime later she returned and told Annie that the matron could see her now.

"Come quickly, Matron Lansdowne does not have all day."

Annie hurried after the attendant and soon found herself facing the matron who was seated behind her desk with her head down, writing. As Annie entered the room, she looked up.

"What is it, Annie?" she asked.

"Matron, I need to talk to you about one of the attendants, Sheila Murphy. She has been very cruel to my friend Mabel. And since I asked her to stop hurting Mabel, she has been harassing me and finding fault with everything I do."

The matron frowned. Her stern look caused Annie to wonder whether she had done the right thing by coming to make her complaint. It was quite obvious that the matron was not used to the women complaining about their treatment.

"Annie, you need to understand that life in here is not easy for the attendants either. You cannot just tell tales every time you feel a little uncomfortable. The attendants are here to help you. If you do something wrong, they must caution you."

Annie thought for a moment. Should she continue or should she just leave well enough alone? She felt she had to say more.

"But it was more than that, Matron. She pulled Mabel's hair and put her arm around her neck. Mabel was in tears and struggling to breathe. She is a tough girl who has lived on the street. She is not easily upset, but she was very distressed."

"As I said, discipline is important in here, Annie. Sometimes the attendants will need to use some force to ensure you all remain safe. You may go now."

Annie frowned. She could not believe that the matron had dismissed her complaint so easily. She was angry as she left the room, but she was beginning to understand that there was little she could do to stand up for herself or anyone else in this awful place.

Chapter Thirteen

As the door closed behind Annie, Elsie Lansdowne sighed. She had just returned to work after her day off. That morning she had locked the door of her cosy cottage, knowing she had to face the world and the asylum again. As she walked through the streets of Kew, she noticed the greengrocers unloading their vegetables fresh from the market, ready for the day's trade. The lamplighter was extinguishing the lamps. The newsboy waved his newspapers over his head and called out the headlines. Elsie hurried on, knowing she would be late if she dawdled.

Now she was back at her desk and the first thing she had to deal with was a complaint. As she thought about what Annie had told her, her face softened. She liked the girl and hated having to be so strict with the inmates. But equally, she knew she had to provide unequivocal support for her attendants. The place would descend into chaos if all the inmates thought they could complain about their treatment. However, it was against Elsie's nature to be so unfair.

Elsie sighed again. She supposed she would need to speak with Sheila, so she went into the dayroom to find her. Sheila was busy assisting with dinner, so Elsie asked her to come to her office as soon as she was free. Sheila had frowned at the interruption.

Elsie paced anxiously back and forth, twisting her wedding band around her finger, as she waited for Sheila to appear. Sheila could be bad-tempered and Elsie knew she would not take news of a complaint well. She was not looking forward to confronting her and was rehearsing what she would say. Soon there was a knock on the door. Elsie returned to her desk, sat down and took a deep breath before she called for Sheila to enter.

"Please sit down, Sheila."

Sheila, looking nervous but defiant, pulled up a chair and sat waiting for Elsie to explain why she had summoned her.

"I have had a complaint, Sheila."

Sheila's face paled. "What do you mean? What about?"

"You supposedly mistreated one of the inmates by pulling her hair and choking her."

"Oh, Matron Lansdowne, you know how difficult they can be. Sometimes a little force is required in order to subdue them."

"Yes, Sheila, I definitely do understand. But I am told that you placed your arm around her neck to restrain her?"

"I had to. She was trying to strike me."

"Are you quite sure of that? Perhaps she was just trying to protect herself. She may have been struggling to breathe with a stranglehold around her neck."

Sheila was breathing hard, and her face was flushed.

"I work hard, Matron Lansdowne. I don't deserve to be harassed over the way I look after the inmates."

Elsie took a deep breath, wondering how to proceed. She knew that the attendants' conditions were poor. They worked long hours and a humble housemaid received a higher wage.

"Look, Sheila, I understand the pressure you and the other attendants are under. But you really must watch how you treat the inmates. However, I am not going to take this any further. I trust you will take note of our discussion today and be more restrained with your care."

Despite her anger, Sheila was grateful.

"Thank you Matron. I will remember," she said through gritted teeth. "This job is all I have. I cannot survive without it."

"I know Sheila. There is not much work available in these difficult times. So I know you will be more careful in the future. You may return to your duties now."

As the door closed behind Sheila, Elsie breathed a sigh of relief. She was grateful that the difficult conversation had been taken care of and she hoped she would not have to address it again. But then she knew it was not an easy job, working with depraved women. She realised she would be presented with this scenario again in the future. Many people were out of work because of the depression, but even still, being an attendant at a mental asylum was a lowly job, and many of them were simply not suited to the work. Elsie knew that although alcohol consumption was not allowed, many of the attendants resorted to it to cope with the pressures of the job.

Elsie's thoughts returned to Annie. She had hoped that Annie would stay out of trouble, but she was doubtful. She was an impetuous young thing, and Elsie was worried for her. From their first interaction, Annie had reminded her of her own daughter. Viola had had a similar impetuous nature. They were even a little bit similar in looks. Viola's hair often became unruly and escaped its pins, as Elsie had noticed with Annie. Although Annie was a naïve country girl, she had the same determined look as Viola in her eyes.

Sometimes Elsie wished she could go back to her earlier life when, despite the abuse she endured, things were so much simpler. But she had lost the one precious thing in her life and there was no going back.

Elsie's married life had not always been unhappy. She and James had been young and desperately in love. Although Elsie's mother had warned her that James came from a volatile family background, and may not always be as patient and caring as he seemed, Elsie would not be put off. She knew he would have little to offer her but she loved him and thought that this would be enough. She and James were married.

At first everything was idyllic, with James paying her every attention and working hard to provide for her. He worked as a farm labourer, which was not a well paid job, so they had little in the way of material things. But they were happy. Elsie enjoyed making a home for them in their small, rented cottage.

But the situation had quickly deteriorated when Elsie happily announced that she was pregnant. James had been furious. Elsie was dumbstruck. She had no idea that he didn't want children. She had never seen him so angry.

"How are we supposed to afford a baby? We barely have enough to provide for ourselves. We can't possibly have another mouth to feed. You must get rid of it."

Elsie stared at him, not quite able to believe that the words had come from his mouth.

"You can't mean that. This is your own flesh and blood."

"Oh, I most certainly do mean it."

Elsie had turned and left the room not wanting to discuss it any further. She was devastated but she knew she could never do anything to harm the baby growing inside her.

As the months went by and the birth approached, James became angrier. Elsie hoped that once the baby was born he would come around. *He is a good man* she thought.

But when the baby was born James had not fallen in love with his tiny daughter as Elsie had hoped. Elsie soon discovered that James Lansdowne would never be a good father. As his daughter grew, he had little patience with her excitable temperament and from her early childhood, he had no time for her. He began to drink, and it wasn't long before his drinking spiralled out of control. Elsie dreaded him coming home each night.

He would come in late, reeling and reeking of spirits. Elsie would make sure that their small home was tidy, and that there was a meal ready for him. If anything angered him, he would fly into a violent rage and he had been known to raise his hand to her. Elsie had made sure to keep Viola out of his way when he was in one of his rages. But that wasn't always possible and on occasions, she also bore the brunt of his anger. She would cower in the corner of the kitchen. This tore Elsie apart. It was one thing being struck and abused herself, but quite another for her to allow him to hit their daughter.

As she got older, Viola soon realised it was better not to be within his reach when he was drunk and angry. But this just meant that he took his anger out on Elsie. Elsie knew that Viola could hear the commotion from her room when James was in one of his tempers. But she was pleased that Viola took heed of her demands that she not try to do anything to help her mother. She had convinced Viola that there was nothing she could do to help so she must stay out of harm's way. Their lives were a living hell.

Elsie was determined Viola would not make the same mistakes that she had made. She should have taken her mother's advice and not married this man despite the fact that she had truly loved him. Women had to be stronger. In fact, Viola didn't have to marry at all if she didn't want to.

When Viola returned from school each day Elsie would help her with her reading and arithmetic. Then they would sit and read the newspaper.

"Viola, look there is another letter from one of the suffragists. We owe so much to these women who are fighting for our rights."

By now Viola was a feisty young girl of fourteen and thanks to Elsie's tutelage, had developed strong ideas about the women's movement.

"Let me read it please." She was silent for some moments as she digested the words.

"I hate men," she said, her face stormy. "Why are they so determined to put us down? They are just afraid of us."

"Oh no, Viola, that is not the way to think," said Elsie. "You must try not to hate anyone. But I agree that men are quite afraid to let women have more say. They have had all the power for so long and they are not willing to let it go. We need to show them that women are capable of making sound decisions too."

"Well, I do hate my father," she said. Elsie sighed. Viola certainly had reason to hate her father.

Suddenly Viola's eyes lit up. "We should go to a meeting mother."

Elsie felt a sense of pride that her young daughter was developing a passion for women's rights.

"That sounds like a very good idea. But we would need to be very careful. If your father found out we would be in terrible trouble."

"We have to stand up for ourselves mother, and this is one way to do that."

"Very well, we will watch the papers and find out when there is an opportunity. But now we must make sure the dinner is ready for when your father gets home. Then you must go to your room until he is asleep."

In desperation, Elsie knew she needed to do something to try to lift both her and her daughter out of this untenable situation. But what could she do that would not anger him further? She sat at the kitchen table reading the paper that she had purchased that morning with her meagre housekeeping money. Suddenly an advertisement caught her eye. There was to be a meeting of the Women's Christian Temperance Union. She wondered if she could make some excuse to James which would allow her and Viola to attend the meeting. But what if James found out? She could not think of that. This was something she had to do for herself and her daughter.

Eventually she had it all planned. When James arrived home from work she had his dinner ready.

"James, I hope you don't mind but Viola and I have promised to visit a friend this evening."

At least James was not intoxicated. "Who are you going to see?" he demanded.

"It is just an old friend; I don't think you would know her. We worked together as nurses before I was married."

When he did not respond, she took his dinner from the oven and put it on the table hoping he would not notice her shaking hands.

She slipped out of the kitchen and went to Viola's room.

"Are you ready?"

"Yes," answered Viola. "Are you sure he won't get angry if we leave the house?"

"Well I can never be sure, but if we slip out quietly now, hopefully he won't take any notice." They stepped out of the room and walked quickly down the passageway and out the front door, closing it quietly behind them.

They walked swiftly to the station and caught a train into the city. They entered the hall and were surprised to see so many women in attendance. They appeared to be from all walks of life. It was such an uplifting experience for both of them and made it slightly easier to deal with the horrendous situation they both faced at home, knowing they were joining the fight for women's rights and that one day things might be better for women in their situation.

Then suddenly their whole world was completely ripped apart. Elsie knew James despised his daughter, but lately he had become obsessed with the belief that, in fact, Viola was not his daughter. He accused Elsie of having an affair. Nothing could be further from the truth. Elsie had loved her husband when they had first married. She would never have strayed. And as time went on and her love for him diminished as he maltreated her, she would not have dared to take a lover. She was too afraid of him to make a wrong move.

But he would not be swayed in his belief. No matter what Elsie said, she could not convince him she had always been faithful.

"She cannot stay in this house," he shouted. "She is not a child of mine. I will not have her under my roof."

He had come home drunk and in a violent rage. Elsie had just served his meal, but now she shrank away from him. He had never before spoken of turning her out.

"What do you mean? She is our child. She is barely sixteen years of age. Where would you expect her to go?"

His face reddened, and she could see that her words had angered him. She rarely answered him back.

"How dare you speak out against me! She is not our child. She belongs to you and the man you allowed to bed you."

Elsie tried to stay calm. "That is not true. I have never been unfaithful."

"I don't believe you. In any case, I have made my decision. You have no say in the matter."

Elsie was not sure what he meant, but the next day she was to find out.

Elsie knew he would not be in good shape when he awoke the next morning, but he had not forgotten his threat.

"Pack your bag, Viola. You cannot stay in this house any longer."

Viola shot her mother a frightened look.

"What do you mean father? this is my home."

"Not anymore it isn't. You will come with me."

Viola's eyes darted from her father to her mother, but she knew better than to disobey James. Sometimes when he was drunk, it was just a matter of steering clear of him. But when he was stone-cold sober, and what's more hungover, experience told her it was best to obey him. So she turned from the room and went to pack a bag. As she left the room, she looked at her mother. She did not need to say anything. The plea for help was clear on her face.

"What are you doing? Where do you think you are taking her? She is my daughter too. You can't just turn her out."

"I have no intention of just turning her out on the streets. "

"Well, where are you taking her?"

As Viola came back into the room, her father answered this question.

"She is not well. She needs to be in hospital."

"What? That is ridiculous. She is perfectly well."

"That is enough Elsie. You have no further say in the matter."

Viola had turned white and wondered if her mother would be able to rescue her this time. Her father grabbed her by the arm. She struggled, but to no avail. He had a firm grip on her and began to drag her from the house.

Elsie was becoming hysterical. She grabbed her husband's arm. He momentarily let go of Viola and struck Elsie across the side of the head with enough force to knock her to the ground. Viola screamed.

Elsie looked at Viola, begging her to run from her father. But Viola appeared frozen to the spot and soon he had grabbed her again and was forcing her from the house. Through the fog caused by the blow to her head, Elsie saw him drag their daughter from their home. She knew Viola was too afraid to resist, as she had borne the brunt of his beatings in the past.

When James returned without their daughter, Elsie was distraught. Her eyes were red-rimmed from crying. She had hoped that his was an empty threat and that he would return with Viola, but it appeared that he had gone through with it.

"Where is she? Where have you taken her?" said Elsie, her voice shrill with fear and anger.

"She is exactly where she needs to be. I have had her admitted to the mental asylum."

"Oh no, you can't mean that."

"Of course I mean it, you stupid woman."

"But she is not mad. She is completely sane. Why would they accept her without a medical reason to do so?"

"They had no choice. I signed the papers, and that was that."

Elsie's knees gave way and she fell to the floor in a crumpled heap, weeping more bitter tears. But it had no effect on James. He simply took up his work tools and headed for the door.

Once James had left the house, Elsie gathered herself and dried her eyes. She must be strong for her daughter. She must try to see Viola and find out what could be done. She grabbed her hat and handbag and slammed the door behind her.

She made her way to the tramcar stop and caught a tram to the Kew Lunatic Asylum. She made her way up the long gravel driveway towards the gates. The gate keeper came to ask her what she wanted.

"I need to see someone in authority. My daughter has been committed and I must see her."

"Come through," said the disinterested gatekeeper, and he directed her to the Administration building where she spoke to the woman behind the reception desk.

"Please, you must help me. My husband has had my daughter committed but there is nothing wrong with her. She shouldn't be here."

"We hear that a lot Madame," said the clerk. "But it is unlikely that she will be able to be released now."

"I must speak to someone in authority. There must be something I can do."

"I will see if the superintendent is able to see you. Please take a seat. What is your name?"

"My name is Elsie Lansdowne and my daughter is Viola."

With that, the clerk left the reception area through a door on the left, closing it behind her.

Elsie sat on the edge of the chair for some time before the clerk reappeared.

"The superintendent is quite busy at the moment, but if you are willing to wait, he will see you as soon as he is able."

"Thank you, I will wait."

As the minutes ticked by, Elsie became more frantic, worried that the superintendent would not see her. But suddenly the door opened.

"Please come in, Mrs Lansdowne," he said politely.

He was an imposing figure in his three-piece suit, with a pocket handkerchief and a gold watch chain draped across his chest. He sat down behind his desk and regarded Elsie over the top of his half-rimmed spectacles.

"Please sit down." Elsie's first impression of him was that he was a good-natured man, but she was soon disappointed. "How can I help you?" he asked.

"It's my daughter, Viola. My husband has signed the papers to have her committed, but there is nothing wrong with her. She is perfectly sane."

"Well, I doubt that Mrs Lansdowne. Our Doctors are very thorough with their examinations. She must have shown signs of madness."

"Well, I expect she may have seemed a little hysterical. She would have been frightened out of her wits."

"All the same, Madam, there is little we can do now. The paperwork has been signed, and the Doctor has made his diagnosis. So until she has calmed down and recovered her wits, she will be forced to stay here."

Elsie looked at him with tears rolling down her face, although she wondered that she had any tears left. She realised that, at least for the moment, she was defeated.

"May I see her at least?"

"No, I am sorry that is not possible. She will need time to settle in and visitors can be unsettling in the first few days. Perhaps if you return again in a week or two."

Elsie could not believe her ears. She rose unsteadily to her feet and stumbled out of the office. She made her way home and collapsed on her bed. There was nothing she could think to do for Viola, so what was the use of living?

Chapter Fourteen

A nnie had tried to stay away from Sheila since she had spoken to Matron Lansdowne. She was more than a little afraid that she had stirred up a hornet's nest. She kept her head down and did her work diligently. However, it was not long before Sheila began to make Annie's life miserable.

Annie was kneeling in the herb garden enjoying the strong scent of mint and rosemary, her mind drifting back to her home. She dug out the weeds with her trowel and piled them up beside her, ready to place in the compost pile. This was work that she loved, clearing the weeds from around the plants so that they had room to grow when the warmer weather came. It really took her mind off her situation and the mounting realisation that there was little chance of escaping this place.

Suddenly, she was shoved roughly from behind so that she fell face first into the garden. She turned around to see Sheila glowering at her angrily. Annie looked around and realised there was no one else close by. Sheila had obviously picked her moment.

"I know it was you who reported me to the matron," Sheila said.

Annie could tell that she was in a fine temper, so she decided that the best course of action was to remain calm and try not to do anything to make Sheila angrier.

"I am sorry, but I was worried that Mabel could not breathe. You were choking her."

"She was perfectly alright. I did not hurt her. You lunatics need to be kept in line and sometimes we need to use force."

"I am not a lunatic. You know that." Annie felt bile rising in her throat as her anger rose. But she knew she must remain calm. She did not want Sheila to get the better of her.

"Well, that is debatable. Why are you in here if you are not mad?"

"Look, I am sorry. I know you have a job to do, but I just think that Mabel was not doing anything wrong. She dropped the pillowcases by accident. I don't think you needed to be so rough with her."

Sheila leaned in close to Annie so that their noses were almost touching. Annie could smell spirits on her breath and could see the contempt and fire in her eyes. She felt real fear now. She shrank away and started to shake.

"I have told you before not to answer me back. You had better watch yourself. I can have you sent to the refractory ward, you know."

"Matron Lansdowne would never allow that."

"Oh, so you think you are some sort of favourite. Well, we will see about that."

And with that, Sheila turned on her heel and stalked off.

Annie sat back on her heels and breathed deeply to try to calm her racing heart. Sheila's threats alarmed her and she was left wondering what she might do next. She was terrified that Sheila would carry out her threat.

Annie had lately taken to playing the piano in the day room. At first she could not bear to look at it because it just reminded her of home. But gradually she had decided that trying to ignore it was not helping. One day she opened the lid on the battered old piano and gently picked out a few notes of one of her favourite pieces, The Nutcracker by Tchaikovsky. It was a complex piece, but she had spent many weeks mastering it, as she loved it so much. The piano was badly out of tune, but the melody was at least recognisable. Annie sat down on the piano stool and began to play. Now, whenever she sat down at the piano, a crowd of women would soon gather around. She played cheerful tunes that the women could dance and sing along to.

Suddenly, her playing was interrupted as Mabel ran screaming into the room. She threw herself on the floor, scratching at her eyes and pulling her hair.

Annie stared at her in horror. What had happened? Her usually calm and happy friend seemed to have completely lost control. Her face was the colour of an overripe plum as she held her breath for long periods of time and her eyes bulged from her head.

Annie raced over to her.

"Whatever is the matter, Mabel?"

"They can't do this to me," shrieked Mabel. "It's not possible."

The attendants took no notice, presumably they knew why Mabel was in such a state. Annie felt she would not get any sense out of her friend until she was able to calm her. So she sat on the floor and tried to comfort her. She could not hug her as Mabel was throwing herself around wildly, so she just tried to provide a comforting touch wherever she could. She was eventually able to get through to Mabel and the uncontrolled thrashing slowed enough so that Annie could hold and comfort her on the floor.

All the other women had gathered around them to see what the commotion was about. Some had fear in their eyes, whilst some of the more disturbed women cackled to themselves as they looked on, apparently thinking this was grand entertainment. Helena appeared at Annie's side as she tried to comfort Mabel.

"She has been told she is well enough to be released," said Helena. Annie was distraught. She knew what this would mean to her friend.

"But they know she has nowhere to go," said Annie. "If they release her, she will just be back on the streets again, being battered and abused."

Sheila stormed into the room.

"What is all this noise about? Get out of my way, Annie."

Annie did not want to let go of Mabel, and wondered what Sheila would do to her. However, she knew she would be in trouble herself if she did not get out of the way.

"Get up Mabel, what is all the fuss about?"

But Mabel was still hysterical.

"They can't do that to me. I can't leave."

Annie looked at her. Surely they had not decided that Mabel was well enough to leave the asylum.

"I think you need some time in isolation to calm down," said Sheila.

"No, please leave her with me," said Annie. "I am sure I can help her calm down."

"Mind your own business, Annie. Come on Mabel, on your feet." Sheila grabbed Mabel by the arm and tried to haul her to her feet. But Mabel was too distraught to stand.

"Come and help me," said Sheila to another attendant who was standing by. They grabbed an arm each and dragged Mabel away as Annie looked on in horror. But there was little she could do. She knew her last complaint had fallen on deaf ears. She was beginning to realise that there was nothing she could do to protect herself or any of the other women. But despite knowing there was nothing she could do, at this moment something snapped inside Annie.

"No, No, No. You cannot take her." Annie began to shriek and weep hysterically. "You are being cruel."

Helena, who had been watching on quietly, tried to calm Annie. But Annie hit out at her.

"Leave me alone," she cried as Helena recoiled.

Helena could not believe what she was seeing. Annie, who a few moments ago had seemed completely calm and peaceful, had turned instantly into the very thing she feared most.... someone who belonged in this place.

"Annie please," begged Helena. "Try to calm down."

But Annie just continued to hit out at Helena with wild, uncoordinated movements. One of the random swings of her arm caught Helena on the side of her head.

At that moment, Sheila let go her hold on Mabel. She called to another attendant who had just entered the room.

"Come and help me. Take this woman to the refractory." Mabel was dragged from the room in a completely hysterical state.

Sheila came back to where Helena grappled with Annie, trying to quell her frenzy. By this time, Annie was completely out of control. She seemed to have no idea what she was doing and as Sheila tried to restrain her; she hit out at her too.

Other attendants rushed into the room to assist. They looked stunned at the commotion. Helena looked around her. The scene had descended into chaos. Other women were becoming more and more animated and squabbling with each other. It truly looked like a madhouse for the first time that Helena could remember.

"Quickly, come and help me." The attendants suddenly sprung into action and helped Sheila to restrain Annie. Annie was shoved to the floor and pinned down but she continued to struggle and scream wildly.

Helena came close to Annie and talked to her quietly, trying to calm her.

"You best leave us to deal with this one," said Sheila. "She has already hurt you." Helena brought her hand to her face and looked in disbelief at the smear of blood that came off onto her hand. She would never have believed that Annie would strike her.

"Please," said Helena. "She is just upset. She didn't mean to hurt anyone."

"That's as may be," replied Sheila. "But she is a danger to herself and others, so she will also be going to the refractory ward."

With that, Sheila and the attendants managed to get Annie almost to her feet. By this time, she was beginning to tire, although the screams that troubled Helena so deeply, had not abated. Sheila stood behind Annie and put her arm around her neck whilst two other attendants grabbed an arm each and together they began to drag her from the room. Helena looked on in despair as Annie struggled to breathe.

Just at that moment, Matron Lansdowne entered the dormitory.

"What is going on? What is all this commotion?"

Sheila immediately loosened her hold on Annie.

"She is hysterical, gone quite mad. We are taking her to the refractory. We need to get her to the shower. A few minutes under the cold water will calm her down."

Helena could see the sympathy in Matron Lansdowne's eyes. But despite that, she responded gruffly.

"I see. Very well. Take her away. I will see her later when she has calmed down a bit. I think she may also need sedation."

Sheila could not hide her pleasure at the support from Matron Lansdowne for the course of action she had decided upon. Helena saw the sly smile that crept onto her lips as they continued to drag Annie from the room.

Annie continued to struggle, but to no avail. She was led away by the attendants to the washroom, where the attendants tied her to a chair under the shower. The icy water bit into her and her teeth began to chatter. She had no idea how long she endured this before the attendants felt she was calm enough to be released from her bonds. They ordered her to dress again. She dragged on her underclothes and dress as quickly as her frozen body would allow. They led her away and into a single padded cell, and they locked the door behind her. She slumped to the floor, wrapping her arms around her body to try to still the shivering. After some time, she heard a noise. She looked up and saw that Doctor Woodforde had appeared in her cell with two attendants.

"Hello Annie," he said.

Annie shot him a furious look. "Why have I been locked away in here? I have done nothing wrong."

"Please calm down Annie, I am going to give you something to help you." He turned to the two attendants. "Hold her please."

The attendants once again restrained Annie. This time she submitted to their grip without struggling. All the fight seemed to have gone out of her. There was a sharp prick in her arm as the needle went in. She felt herself relax as the medication spread through her body. Her head felt fuzzy and her mind went blank.

When the Doctor and the attendants left, she cowered in a corner and looked around her. Apart from a bed that rested on the floor and a chair, there were no other furnishings in the room. After some time, she had no idea how long, she felt her head start to clear. Realising she was really alone, she crossed the small room and slumped gratefully onto the bed. Her head gradually stopped spinning as she lay there.

The door opened again and Annie watched fearfully to see who would enter. When she realised it was Matron Lansdowne, she sat up tentatively.

"Hello Annie," said the matron as she quietly entered the room. Behind her, Annie noticed one of the kinder attendants.

For a moment, Annie could only stare at her.

"What is happening to me, Matron Lansdowne? Why have I been locked up?"

"Annie, you attacked another patient and also one of my staff."

"I don't remember," Annie stared wide eyed.

"You really must try to control your temper, Annie. Your friend Helena has rather a nasty gash on her cheek where you hit her."

"Helena? I would never hurt Helena."

"But you did Annie."

Annie was shaken by this information. She only had a vague recollection of losing her temper. She really couldn't even remember what had set her off.

"Now Annie, I am sorry, but you must remain here where you can't hurt anyone else until we are sure that you are feeling better."

Annie lost track of the days she spent in isolation. Each day in the company of two attendants, she would be allowed out of her room to bathe. The only time she saw anyone else was when her food arrived or when Doctor Woodforde came by to administer her medication each day. Annie felt vague and listless.

The Doctor examined Annie with thoughtful eyes. Matron Lansdowne had called him to see if there was anything further that could be done for Annie. After several days in isolation, she was still not responding well. It was only when the Doctor gave her the medication each day that she calmed down. For the rest of the time, she was ill-tempered and vague.

"I believe she needs some more cold water treatment," he said.

"Are you sure Doctor?" asked Elsie. She knew all the inmates dreaded cold water treatment. It was used as a last resort. However, it did seem to calm them down. The Doctor eyed Elsie angrily.

"I hope you are not questioning my decision, Matron Lansdowne?"

"Of course not, Doctor, but it is just that Annie is normally quite well behaved." She knew better than to argue with Doctor Woodforde.

"Well, that's as may be, however at the moment she is certainly not well behaved, as you put it. She needs further treatment, and this is what I have decided. Please arrange it." With that, he left the room.

Elsie looked at Annie. Despite the dull, empty look in Annie's eyes, the result of the recent injection, Elsie could also see the fear that the Doctor's words had evoked.

"Please Matron Lansdowne," Annie's voice was barely audible. "I can't bear to go through that again. I am calm now. I will behave, I promise."

"I am sorry Annie, you know that I have to obey the Doctor's instructions." She called the attendants and gave them instructions and left them to deal with Annie's pleas. She felt guilty that there was nothing she could do, but she hoped that the treatment would indeed work to calm Annie's rage.

Two attendants led Annie to the scullery where the cold bath was being prepared. The bath was filled with iced water and they made Annie remove her clothes. Despite her protests and the fear that built within her, she found she did not have the energy to resist. She gasped as she felt the shock of the water as the attendants forced her down to lie in the freezing water. She could hardly breathe. Once she was stretched out in the bath, the attendants covered the bath so that only Annie's head was visible.

Annie started to shiver uncontrollably. Within minutes, her whole body was numb, and the shivering stopped. She lay immersed in the water for some time until finally the attendants removed the cover and she was allowed to get out. She could barely move and had to be helped from the bath. Her body was blue with cold. The attendants rubbed at her body with rough towels and her skin prickled painfully as the blood flow returned and warmed her limbs. She pulled the thin towel around her shoulders and her teeth chattered madly in her head. Finally, she was able to dress. She knew that whatever the cost, she must do everything in her power to avoid this treatment in the future.

The attendants led her back to the isolation cell. She lay down on the bed and continued to shiver for several hours before her body returned to its normal temperature.

One morning, the door opened and Annie looked for the food that she thought must accompany any visitor to her cell. But instead, two attendants entered her cell with the camisole that she had seen so many other patients wearing. Her foggy brain could not comprehend what was happening as her hands were forced into the locked pockets and the buckles at the back were fastened. The camisole weighed heavily upon her, and she struggled to walk as they led her out into the yard. She blinked as the sunlight burned her eyes. As her eyes adjusted to the brightness, she looked around her to see the other women also out in the yard. She began to walk, listlessly glancing around her, confused and not sure what she was seeing.

"Annie, are you alright?" Annie looked at the woman who had spoken to her. Did she know her? Gradually recognition dawned on her and she realised the woman trying to talk to her was her friend, Helena.

"I don't know," Annie replied. "What has happened to me?"

"Relax Annie, you will be alright. At least they have let you come out for some exercise. That is a good sign."

Annie looked around her, barely recognising that she was in the yard.

"You must be strong, Annie," continued Helena, when Annie made no comment.

"What do you mean?" asked Annie

"You need to stay calm so that they will allow you to leave the refractory ward and come out of isolation."

But Annie was still confused. The medication was making her dull and stupid. Soon the attendants came to lead her back to her cell.

Chapter Fifteen

A nnie felt completely lost. She had lost all track of time and had no idea where she was or what day it was.

The door to her cell opened. Annie forced her eyes open. She was groggy and disoriented. Her head felt heavy as she tried to lift it off the pillow. A woman entered the room and smiled sympathetically at Annie. Through the fog, she could tell the woman's expression held understanding. Annie knew she should recognise her, but her mind was too foggy to recall who it was. She stared at her and struggled to make sense of what she was looking at.

"Hello Annie," said the woman. "How are you feeling? I can see you are much calmer. The medication is having the desired effect."

Annie stared at her blankly, still trying to raise her head.

The woman pulled the chair up beside Annie's bed, sat down and reached for Annie's hand. The touch of her hand barely registered with Annie.

"Come Annie, you know me, don't you? Matron Lans-downe?"

Something pierced the fog in Annie's brain. But she seemed to have forgotten how to talk. She opened her mouth, but no words came out.

"You are going to be alright Annie. If you continue to improve, you will be able to be moved back to the ward soon."

The women's words made little sense to Annie. But it felt good to have some company and to hear some kind words after so long on her own.

"We will start to reduce the medication now."

As the medication was withdrawn, Annie started to feel again. But at first she did not enjoy what she was feeling. Aches and pains racked her whole body and she struggled to sleep. She craved the feeling of oblivion that the drugs had provided and begged the attendants for more when they came to bring her food. She needed to feel the kick from the medication, which made her feel relaxed and helped her to forget her desperate plight. But eventually she began to feel her old self again. She became calmer and her mind started to clear. She noticed the harsh white walls of the isolation cell and heard the footsteps of the attendants as they passed her door.

Now she realised where she was, and the desperation to get out of this lonely room returned. She needed someone to talk to. The attendants delivering her food were still the only people she saw each day, except for the odd times she had been allowed out for exercise, and only the compassionate ones amongst them would take the time to have a brief conversation with her. She had regained her appetite and ate the food hungrily, even though she tried to prolong the eating as a way to pass the time. Slowly, as she came to her senses, she felt like she might go crazy again from the long hours with nothing to occupy her time. At her request, a kindly attendant brought her a book to read, and this offered a small amount of solace for a few hours. But she knew she must get out of here. She had vague memories of the visit from Matron Lansdowne and somehow the words that she needed to stay calm remained at the forefront of her mind. Though her mind was still foggy, she knew that this was the only way that they would release her from her solitary cell, so she redoubled her efforts to be calm and polite to anyone who entered.

Annie heard the key in the lock and turned to see two attendants enter.

"Come Annie, it is time for you to rejoin the others."

Annie stared at the attendants blankly. The attendants became impatient as Annie made no move to leave the cell.

"Hurry up. Don't you want to get out of this cell?"

Annie turned her back to the attendants, expecting to be buckled into the camisole.

"No Annie, you are behaving very well now. You will be allowed back into the ward without your restraints. The Doctor believes you are much better."

Annie turned slowly back to the attendant. Still she could not understand what was happening. She did not struggle as she allowed the attendant to take her by the arm and lead her from the cell and back to the ward. After so many days in isolation, she found the noise and chaos of the other women overwhelming. The attendants led her to the dayroom and left her. She curled herself up into a ball on a chair as the chaos went on around her. As she once again became accustomed to her surroundings, she noticed Catherine working at her embroidery. She did not move from her position but sat staring at Catherine, somehow transfixed by the movement of her needle. She felt the motion and the sameness of the action calm her. But still she felt anxious and could not think clearly. Slowly, she became more accustomed to the noise and chaos once again.

Helena appeared beside her.

"Come Annie," she said. "Come with me into the garden." She gently helped Annie to her feet and guided her out of the dormitory into the yard. Annie peered up at the dull grey sky with clouds skittering across, blocking out much of the sunshine. The trees were bare of leaves, showing their grey skeletons.

As they walked in the fresh air, Annie's head cleared. The wind was high and Annie stared out at the tall fig and pine trees beyond the walls. Further in the distance, she could see the gums that reminded her of the country where she had lived all her life. She longed to be back by the river in Avoca, watching the water flowing swiftly and hearing the song of the frogs and the crickets. Soon the weather would warm up and the daylight would stretch out as the days become longer, which was a welcome prospect for Annie.

"Are you alright Annie?" asked Helena. "You have been on your own for many days. I know what that is like. You must feel very confused. Have they been giving you medication?"

Annie looked at her with dull eyes.

"Yes, but I don't know what. At least it makes me forget. But they have stopped giving it to me now. I wish I could still have it."

"I know, but you are much better off without it Annie, even though it does not feel like that at the moment. If you want to get out of this place, you need to show them you are getting well."

The two women continued wandering around the yard. The air was icy cold, so despite wearing their blue serge coats over their heavy cotton dresses, they needed to keep moving to keep out the cold. The garden was colourless without the summer flowers blooming. Annie reached down to touch the rosemary plant. She picked a piece and held it up to her nose. The aroma was strong. It was good to be out in the fresh air again. She must never do anything to cause them to put her back in the refractory ward.

It took Annie a while to recover from her time in isolation. Helena was constantly by her side helping her to maintain an even temper. But as Annie regained her senses she suddenly realised she really knew very little about this woman who had been her best friend throughout the months of her incarceration.

"Why have you never been released? You have never really told me your story." Annie felt ashamed to admit to herself that she had been so self-obsessed that she hadn't asked before.

The two women were once again out in the yard in the wintery sunshine. Despite the bitingly cold July day, they both stopped and sat on a bench so that Helena could tell her story.

"My husband had me committed," said Helena.

Annie looked at her friend in horror. "What? That is terrible. Why would he do such a thing?"

"Yes, it was not pleasant to think that a man I once loved could do that to me. He was really a good man. But I suppose he had his grievances."

"What could possibly be that bad? You are a wonderful person Helena, and you have been such a good friend to me."

"I had disappointed him. I had not been able to give him a child. He desperately wanted a son to carry on his name. I had many pregnancies, but each of them ended in miscarriage. I could not cope with his expectations and just got sadder and sadder."

"Oh Helena, that is so unfair."

By now, the two women were becoming chilled by the icy wind.

"Come, let's walk again and I will tell you the full story."

As they walked, Helena related the rest of her story.

"I struggled with my feelings for such a long time. Until eventually it all became too much and I tried to end my life."

Annie's eyes widened as she listened in silence to her friend's desperate story.

"I drew a bath and used his razor to cut my wrists. But luckily, although it didn't feel too lucky at the time, my husband came home and found me. They took me to the hospital. After I recovered, he told me he could not deal with me any longer and had me committed. I am not sure that I really blame him. I would not have been a pleasant person to live with."

"Helena, you must not say that. He put too much pressure on you. No wonder you felt depressed and that you could not go on. But you are well now, aren't you? You should not be here. Is there any chance of you being released?"

"I don't know Annie, but I am not in any hurry. You know, I feel a certain level of security being in here. There are no expectations upon me. I suppose that is why I no longer want to end my life. I want to keep living, even if I am locked away from the world."

Annie was thoughtful. Many of the other women were worse off than her. Her own mind was also starting to clear. She was thinking about how she might be able to be released. But she was also starting to understand that there was little point in raging against the authorities. If she was to have any chance of being released, she would need to show that she was of sound mind and that the dangerous thoughts that had brought her here were behind her.

_ee_

Annie was growing stronger with each passing day. She was no longer missing the dulling effects of the medication they had given her whilst in the refractory ward. Now her mind was clearer again, and she noticed more of her surroundings. She was back working in the laundry and garden.

She was making her bed early one morning when Mabel appeared being guided by an attendant. Annie realised with a shock, and no small measure of guilt, that she had barely given Mabel a thought since she had returned to the ward. She looked closely at her friend. Her eyes were dull, and she moved slowly. She sat down heavily on her bed as the attendant left her.

"Mabel, hello, are you alright?" Mabel looked at her vaguely and did not answer. By now, Annie recognised that look. Mabel was drugged and probably didn't even recognise Annie.

Over the next few days, Mabel came to her senses and recognised Annie again. The drugs were wearing off and Mabel was irritable and unsettled. Annie knew that feeling from her own recent withdrawal from the drugs. She patiently put up with Mabel's irritability and helped her to get back to more normal day-to-day activities. But eventually Mabel was back to her old self and Annie could talk to her.

"What happened Mabel? Did the Doctor realise you are not well enough to be released?"

"It is all a bit of a blur really," replied Mabel. "I don't remember much of my time in isolation. I was glad for the drugs to let me stop thinking, but now I feel so much clearer without them."

"But what about your release? They were going to make you leave."

"Well, it seems that they have changed their minds, at least for the moment. I guess my reaction when they told me caused them to rethink my release. Matron Lansdowne said that there would be no plans for my release at the moment."

"That is good news then, Mabel. I really feel for you that you have no one on the outside who can help you. I, on the other hand, am desperate to get out of this place."

Chapter Sixteen

Annie sat in the dayroom trying to read. She had found that she could take some comfort from reading. There were few books on the small bookshelf, but Annie had not read many of them, so had found several that interested her. She sat now amongst the usual commotion of the dayroom. At first, she found it almost impossible to concentrate. She had to read the words aloud to help block out the distractions. But eventually the noise faded into the background as she became engrossed in the story and she began to actually take in what she was reading.

"I won't take it," said the woman. Annie looked to the other end of the room where the cry had come from.

"Don't be silly, you must take it. Open your mouth."

"No, I won't."

"We will see about that." Sheila put out her foot and tripped the woman, who fell heavily to the floor on her backside. Sheila moved quickly and shoved the off balance women onto her back and knelt on the woman's chest. By this time, the poor woman was crying out in anguish and struggling madly.

Annie ran to the pair as they struggled.

Another attendant, presumably hearing the fuss, entered at that moment. As she saw what was going on, she instinctively turned her back. She was much gentler and had treated Annie with kindness.

"Please help her," whispered Annie to the attendant who had just entered. But she simply shrugged her shoulders, indicating there was little she could do.

"Lie still," said Sheila. "If you cooperate, this will be easier on you."

"No, I won't take it. It makes me worse. I cannot think straight when I have it."

"Does she really have to take it?" pleaded Annie. "She has been quite calm."

"Oh, so you are a Doctor now are you?" said Sheila. "Of course she has to have it. The Doctor has prescribed medication, and it is my job to ensure that she takes it."

She put the spoon to the poor woman's lips. But the woman kept her mouth clamped tightly shut. The attendant continued to push the spoon into the woman's lips. The woman's face contorted in pain.

"Please, you are hurting her," said Annie. "Can't you please just let her up? Maybe I can convince her to take the medication if you stop hurting her." But Sheila ignored Annie's pleas.

"I don't have time for this nonsense." Shiela continued to push the spoon into the woman's mouth until suddenly blood appeared on her lip. "Don't just stand there. Come and help me," she said to the other attendant.

Unable to ignore the situation any longer, the other attendant knelt beside Sheila and forced the woman's mouth open. She gagged as the liquid caught in her throat, but finally it was done and the two attendants let go of her. Sheila stormed out of the room. The distraught woman lay on the floor sobbing. Annie and the attendant helped her up and led her to her bed. The attendant fetched a cloth and a basin of water and left Annie to bathe the woman's lip.

"I am so sorry," said Annie. "I really tried to help. But there was really nothing I could do. Are you alright?"

The woman looked at Annie.

"Thank you for trying. I really hate the medication. I wish they wouldn't make me take it." As she spoke, her voice slurred as the medication took effect.

Annie smiled gently.

"Just try to rest now," she whispered as the woman slipped into a fitful sleep.

Not long after Mabel returned to the ward, she and Annie were sitting in the dayroom. Annie was trying to read, but the distractions today just seemed too overwhelming. She felt unsettled and wanted to lose herself in a book, but was unable to do so.

Mabel had been idly chatting at intervals. She was back to her old self but always on the alert. Both of the young women hoped Mabel would never again be told that they would release her from the asylum.

"Have you heard the news, Annie?" asked Mabel.

"What news is that?" said Annie patiently, wishing that her friend would stop chatting so that she might read her book.

"Someone from the men's ward escaped last night."

Annie's eyes rose from her book and she began to take an interest in what Mabel was saying. This was news indeed. In all the time she had been here, she hadn't heard of anyone escaping.

"Surely not, Mabel? That could not be possible."

"Well, I heard the attendants talking about it, so it must be true."

"What did they say?"

"They did not seem sure about how he was able to get through the locked gates. Perhaps someone made a mistake and left the gates unlocked. But he has been found and returned. Apparently, he is making much of the fact that he just walked out of the gates. Someone must have slipped up."

"Someone will probably be in trouble for that. Have you ever heard of anyone else escaping Mabel?"

"Oh yes, there have been a number of people who have escaped whilst I have been here."

"Really? It seems so improbable when there are so many locked doors and gates that anyone could ever escape."

"Yes, it really makes you wonder, but somehow people do manage. Although usually they are found quickly and brought back."

Annie was feeling a lot stronger now. Her confusion had abated. She decided it was time for action. There must be something she could do to advance her cause. She wondered about her father. He had still not contacted her. After the letter from Rosa had arrived, she had hoped that he would come to see her. But still, she had heard nothing from him. She made up her mind to write to him herself. Perhaps a letter from her might convince him she was well enough to be released. She approached the attendant who had always been kind to her, and asked for a pen and some paper. The attendant returned some time later and gave Annie the writing tools.

"What do you want them for?" asked the attendant.

"I am going to write to my father."

"Take care what you write, Miss Annie," said the attendant. "Matron Lansdowne reads all the letters. It will not be posted unless she approves it."

"Thank you for the warning," replied Annie.

She took the pen and paper, thanking the attendant, and sat on her bed. She thought carefully before she wrote. Although she still felt anger towards her father, she knew it would do no good to berate him. She began to write, choosing her words carefully. She was not sure she would be given more paper if she did not get it right the first time.

23rd July 1894

Dear Father,

I hope you and the family are well. I am very sorry for causing you and mother grief. I am quite well now and would very much like to return home. People in here have been kind to me and I have made some good friends, in particular a lovely woman named Helena. She has helped me a lot and has made me see the error of my ways.

I don't know what to do. I need your help. I have been locked away in here for months. But I am feeling much more myself now.

I have been well treated. The attendants here are mostly very kind. But I do not need to be here anymore. Please say you will vouch for me and request that I be released. Surely you do not think that I need to stay here indefinitely? Please come and get me.

I remain your obedient daughter,

Annie.

It was a brief letter. Annie did not know how else to implore her father to help her. She folded the letter and gave it to the attendant.

"Please, can you let me know whether it has been approved and posted?"

"I am sorry, Miss Annie, but I won't be able to do that. Matron Lansdowne will not tell me if it gets posted. You will just have to hope that you get a reply."

Chapter Seventeen

E lsie paced the floor of her office. Her thoughts were troubled. Since joining the suffragists in campaigning for women's franchise she had been so much more aware of the restrictions that were placed on women. She had no control over her daughters fate when her husband had Viola committed. Elsie also realised that her position as matron allowed very little power to influence the lives of the inmates. The Doctors were the only ones who had the capacity to make real decisions. She held Annie's letter in her hand. Annie definitely seemed much improved and since they had released her from the refractory ward, she had not caused any trouble. Now was the time Elsie must stand up for her beliefs and intervene on Annie's behalf. Whilst she still had faith in the system and knew that some women needed to be held here, she also knew there were many who had recovered and should be released.

The dormitories were overcrowded. If only the Medical Board would take a more compassionate approach. They came to visit the asylum on a monthly basis, but it was really only a cursory inspection. If they looked more closely, they would see that the overcrowding could be lessened by releasing some of the inmates who had recovered. It was up to Elsie and the rest of the staff to help these women under less than optimal conditions. The budget was ever tightening and resources were stretched to the limit. The depression continued to bite.

Elsie chewed her lip and wondered what to do. After some minutes of careful consideration, she took a piece of paper from her drawer and began to write. She would add her own letter to Annie's father providing her opinion that Annie had recovered enough to be released.

As she thought about how best to approach her missive to Annie's father, she recalled with sadness that she had not been able to convince her own husband to have mercy on Viola. Now she was completely alone. Both her daughter and husband were dead. But she mourned only one of them. She could not avoid slipping back into the terrible memory of losing her daughter.

Elsie had continued to visit the asylum every day until eventually she had been allowed to see her daughter. Now she was permitted to visit once a week. She had to be careful, though. If James found out, she knew he would fly into one of his rages. Each time Elsie saw her daughter, Viola was completely distraught. It broke Elsie's heart.

"Mother, surely there must be something you can do? You know I shouldn't be here." Her words were filled with anguish and seeing the desperation in her daughter's eyes brought Elsie to tears.

"I am so sorry, Viola. If only there were more I could do. I should have been able to protect you, my darling. It is all my fault."

"Oh no, mother, I am not blaming you. My father is beastly."

"Yes, I know. But I have pleaded with him. I don't have the authority to influence your release. All I can do is continue to try to convince him. But you know, most of the time he is intoxicated. When he is drunk it is impossible to get through to him." Her voice trembled with despair as her tears overflowed.

Elsie did not add that if she did try to broach the subject of Viola's release when James had been drinking, he would fly into a violent rage and she would end up battered and bruised. Viola did not need to know that. She never visited her daughter when there were any signs of the abuse that James meted out. As far as Viola knew, the beatings had mostly stopped. And it was better that she continued to believe that.

Viola's happy and kind nature faded as she spent more time in the asylum. Her spirit was broken as she became more and more withdrawn. Elsie could see that she was losing weight, and the shine had gone out of her eyes. The only saving grace was that at least she was safe from her father's abuse.

But then early in 1890, when Viola had been in the asylum for over a year, the Russian Flu hit. All over the world, people were dying from this new influenza. There was no way to stop it from getting into institutions and soon many inmates of the asylum were infected. Elsie was no longer allowed to visit. But she would not be deterred, and came to the reception desk daily and asked to see Viola.

"Please, you must let me see her," she begged.

"I am sorry, Mrs Lansdowne, but we cannot allow anyone in. It is too dangerous."

"Can you at least tell me if my daughter is well?"

"She has contracted influenza, but she is not in a serious condition."

Elsie was distraught. There was no way of knowing whether her daughter was receiving the treatment she would need to fight off the deadly illness. In her deteriorated condition, Elsie was afraid that Viola would not have the strength to recover.

She continued to check in every day until the fateful day when she learned her daughter had succumbed to the disease.

Once again, she arrived at the Administration desk.

"How is my daughter?"

By now, all the clerks knew Elsie well. They looked at each other, not wanting to be the one to break the news.

"I am so very sorry, Mrs Lansdowne, but Viola passed away this morning."

Elsie felt her knees buckle, and a strangled cry escaped from her throat.

"It can't be," she whispered as she slumped to the floor. The clerks did not know what to do. There was really little they could do. They had had to deliver this news to many family members over the last few months. One kind clerk came out from behind the desk and helped Elsie to her feet and guided her to a chair. She called to the other clerk to get a cup of tea. As Elsie sipped the hot sweet tea, the clerk tried to offer what comfort she could.

"Really, we are very sorry for your loss, but there is not a lot that can be done for those who catch the Russian Flu. Many have died."

"Where is she? I must see her."

"That is not possible. They have taken her to the morgue. You will have to ask the authorities there."

Elsie was deep in shock as she left the asylum. She did not know where to turn. But her determination that her daughter be given a Christian burial strengthened her resolve. She knew she would have to draw on every ounce of inner strength that she had in order to face her husband. She had to convince him that this was the right thing to do. As she drew close to their home, she braced herself for the inevitable confrontation with James. Her anger was building, and she was slightly buoyed by the knowledge that payday was a couple of days away. James would have little money to spend at the pub. So she hoped he would not be drunk when he arrived home that evening.

After taking to her bed and shedding bitter tears for some hours, she summoned her strength to prepare his meal as normal. When he arrived home and came into their small kitchen, she was relieved to see that although he was in a foul mood, he had indeed not been drinking. As she served up his meal, she broke the news to him.

"James, I have something to tell you."

"Well, out with it, woman. What is it?"

"It's Viola."

"What about her? You know I don't want to know anything about her. She is lost to me as a daughter."

"That is one thing you are right about, James. She is indeed lost to both of us."

"Yes, she is securely locked in a place where she cannot be a nuisance."

"No, James, she is not. She died in the early hours of this morning of the Russian Flu."

James sat motionless, his face pale. Elsie could see that despite his professed abhorrence of his daughter, her death meant something to him.

But he recovered his bluster quickly.

"I don't see what you think I can do about that."

"We should give her a decent Christian burial."

"We can't afford that," he said quickly.

"But you won't stand in my way of arranging a funeral."

"Do what you like, but you can leave me out of it. And don't expect me to fork out any money."

This was enough for Elsie. To know that she could arrange a funeral for Viola without his interference was a relief. He did not know that she had been saving small amounts of the housekeeping money for a long time and she hoped this would be enough to provide a decent funeral for her daughter.

Now that she had handled that, all her strength left her and she locked herself in the bedroom and collapsed on the bed and gave full vent to her grief.

The funeral was arranged. It was a dreary day as Elsie dressed in her mourning attire. She had dyed one of her dresses, as she could not afford to buy something black to wear. Even purchasing the small bottle of dye had stretched her budget. Elsie had managed to pay for a basic wooden coffin and a plaque to mark Viola's grave. She made her way to the cemetery where the coffin waited. She had not been able to see her darling Viola one last time. The morgue had not allowed it. She felt the unfairness of this keenly. Normally if someone died, they would be laid out in the parlour of the home so that others could say their goodbyes. She supposed it was a forlorn hope in any case, as any friends her poor Viola had, seemed to have deserted her when she was committed to the asylum. So Elsie stood alone at the graveside and listened to the priest give the final blessing. Her tears flowed as the coffin was lowered into the grave. Elsie threw in a small bunch of violets. She had picked them that morning from her own garden, from the patch that she and Viola had planted when she was a small girl, gladdened that they were flowering just at this time.

Things did not improve in the Lansdowne household. James' drinking and rages grew even worse. Elsie could not help but think that he did, in fact, feel some guilt at his treatment of his daughter and was trying to bury his feelings in an alcoholic haze. But he would never admit to it for one moment.

Now that Elsie had only herself to protect, she was careful to do what she could to avoid angering James. His meals were prepared for whenever he arrived home. Once she had served his meal she barricaded herself in Viola's room. No matter how he raged, she did not come out until the house fell silent and she knew that he had passed out.

Elsie had just finished preparing the evening meal when there was a knock at the door. It was payday, and she knew James would be in his worst drunken state when he arrived home, so she needed to make sure there was nothing out of place to upset him needlessly. Not that it really took a lot. He would fly into a rage and beat her at the slightest provocation. The visitor startled Elsie and she hoped that she could get rid of them before her husband arrived home.

She hurried to the front door. Peering through the stained glass paneling, that surrounded the door, she could just see the outline of two people. She nervously opened the door just enough so that she could see her visitors and was shocked to see two police officers standing at her door. They were both big burly men, one rather more rotund and who looked older than the other.

"Are you Mrs Lansdowne?" asked the older of the two police officers.

"Yes, that's right."

"May we come in?"

Elsie moved back and opened the door fully to allow them to enter the hallway, then led them to the sitting room to the left of the hallway.

"Please take a seat. What is it?" asked Elsie with a look of concern. She was sure this meant bad news. As the two police officers sat on her couch, she too took a seat in her chair opposite.

"I am sorry to say we have some rather bad news for you."

Elsie said nothing. Her voice seemed to have left her. The police officer continued.

"Unfortunately, there has been an accident and your husband has been killed. He was leaving the hotel on the corner and was run over by a large carriage. His head was crushed under the wheels and there was nothing that could be done."

Elsie stared and wrung her hands, twisting her wedding ring. She didn't really know how she felt. She had loved her husband once and couldn't help feeling pity that he had met his end in such a gruesome manner.

"Is there someone we can call for you?" said the police officer. Elsie realised there was no one. She had no family and her husband had cut her off from any friendships she might once have had. She was on her own.

"No, there is no one. But I will be alright. Thank you for your concern."

"He was taken to the local hospital so you can contact them to make any arrangements. If there is anything we can do, please let us know. You can reach us at the local police station."

"Thank you. You have been very kind."

She showed the two men out and went to the kitchen to make herself a cup of tea, to which she added an extra spoonful of sugar. She took the tea back to her sitting room and slumped into her chair.

Could this really be true? She could not believe that she was finally free of him. An amazing sense of relief overcame her. There had been no love between her and her husband for many years, but now she was free of him, of his torment and violence. It was as if someone had literally lifted a great weight from her shoulders. She could hardly believe it. As a Christian woman these feelings were quite alien to her and she felt guilty. But her life had been hell for so long, she felt God would forgive her.

So many emotions were swirling around in her mind. But the overwhelming emotion was sadness. Why had her life turned out this way? She had loved Viola dearly and had always tried so hard to please her husband. Now she had nothing.

The funeral went ahead on a frosty day in the dead of winter. Elsie stood shivering in her black mourning dress, surrounded by cold grey gravestones, monuments to the dead. Once again, she was the only mourner standing by the grave as the priest read the last rites. This surprised her a little, as she had expected that at least some of his workmates might have attended. Perhaps he was as unpleasant to them as he had been to her and their daughter. At the conclusion of the service, she thanked the priest and walked slowly towards her daughter's grave. Bitter tears ran down her cheeks and the words on the plaque that showed the dates spanning Viola's short life blurred. If only she had managed to free Viola from the asylum, perhaps her death would have been prevented and her life would not have been cut so miserably short. As she walked away from the cemetery, her thoughts turned to what would happen next.

Over the previous few days, whilst making preparations for the funeral, an idea had begun to form in Elsie's mind. Many hours had been spent pondering how she would support herself now that James had died. There was little enough left of her savings after paying for two funerals. Before her marriage, Elsie had been a nurse. It had been an enjoyable job that had also paid well enough. It had been a disappointment to her, to have to leave her job to get married. Now Elsie wondered if it was possible to return to this life.

But not just as a nurse. Knowing the conditions that Viola had had to endure in the asylum, Elsie wondered if this was a pathway she should pursue. Perhaps there was something she could do to ensure that the women at the asylum were treated in a more humane way.

It took Elsie some time to gather herself and recover after the shocks and losses she had endured. But she was a strong woman. She knew she must move on with her life.

Attending meetings of the Women's Christian Temperance Union even when Viola had been incarcerated in the asylum had given her some comfort. Despite her heavy heart at that time and not having any power to do anything to get her daughter released, the meetings had provided hope that eventually women would have more choices and be able to make decisions for themselves. Now that there was nothing standing in her way, she was determined to step up her work with the suffrage movement.

But she also had to earn a living. After spending what she considered to be a decent length of time mourning her husband, she visited the asylum.

It was pleasing that the clerk on duty was someone she had met when Viola was incarcerated. Although she felt unsure about this course of action, the familiarity of this caring woman behind the desk put some of her fears to rest as she approached the desk.

"Hello, I wonder if I would be able to speak to the superintendent."

"Oh hello, Mrs Lansdowne," said the clerk. "How lovely it is to see you. I hope you are well. We were so sorry for your loss."

"Thank you."

"I will see if the superintendent has time to speak with you."

The clerk soon returned and directed her through to the superintendent's office. After a brief discussion during which Elsie assured the rather pompous man that she was a qualified nurse, the superintendent was pleased to sign her up as an attendant. The attendants that he usually had to employ were often not of a very high standard, given that the wage offered by the asylum was so low.

Elsie soon settled into the role and when the position of matron of the women's wing became vacant, she was the obvious choice. Elsie began to feel that she had partly recovered her life. She would never get over the loss of her daughter, of course, but her grief had changed as she involved herself in the business of looking after the women in the asylum.

She found it hard to implement any improvements, though. Funding was an issue, but also the superintendent and the Doctors gave little credence to her opinions. Although, funnily enough, she noticed on a couple of occasions that small suggestions she had made came to be implemented with credit given to the male staff. There must be something that could be done.

It was Elsie's day off. She dressed carefully and caught the train into the city and walked the final few blocks to the headquarters of the Women's Christian Temperance Union.

The meeting was addressed by a woman Elsie had not seen at the meetings before. Elsie was rather surprised when she took the floor. She was dressed in a rather dowdy fashion and so did not create the impression of a powerful suffragist.

"My name is Annette Bear and I have recently returned to Victoria. I believe that the enfranchisement of women would be conducive to the highest national welfare and I am sure you would all agree."

"The vote would be the most effective instrument for improving conditions of life," she said.

The speaker paused here as murmurs of ascent and polite clapping filled the room. Annette Bear continued.

"You will no doubt be aware that most things worth having were originally produced by women."

Elsie drew breath. That seemed like a very bold statement.

Annette smiled and went on. "But on a more serious note, it seems I am just in time for an exciting development. The ground work has been done and it is now time to approach the government with our demands. Jane Munro, who you will all know from previous meetings, is the wife of the Premier, James Munro. She suggested that we make a deputation to the Premier, which we have done. The Premier informed us that in order for him to take any action on the matter there would need to be a united and representative agitation on the part of women."

"I propose that we start a petition. We will travel all over Victoria, if need be, to collect signatures from women from all walks of life, country and city and present our case to the government. We do not have a lot of time so we will need help from all here present."

Now there was loud applause from the assembled women. Elsie felt a prickle of excitement. This woman was a powerful orator. Would she be able to make a real difference to the plight of women?

"If you are willing to volunteer to collect signatures for the petition, please add your name to the list."

Elsie gladly added her name. Over the next six weeks she and many other women travelled by train all over the countryside to collect signatures.

On the 29 September 1891, the petition containing over 30,000 signatures was tabled in parliament.

Elsie sat in the public gallery and could not contain her pride when the monster roll of paper was carried into the chamber by several men.

Chapter Eighteen

Several weeks had passed since Annie had penned the letter to her father and still she had heard nothing from him. In fact, she actually had no way of knowing whether the letter had even been posted. She still could not believe that her father had abandoned her.

Annie and Helena shared all their worries. They were sitting in the garden on a chilly day in early spring. The deciduous trees were showing tinges of green. The garden was dull under the wintery sun. But Annie was pleased that spring was not far away. Soon the gardens would be awash with the flowers of the seedlings they had recently planted. Both women loved flowers, so were keen for the garden beds to again be full of colour and fragrance.

Annie turned to face Helena. "I don't know what to do. I have not heard a word from father. There must be something I can do to get out of here. I know you feel safe here Helena, but I long to get out and be free again."

Helena sighed. "I am beginning to think I am ready to face the world again too, Annie." Annie looked at her friend and smiled at the look of determination on Helena's face. "Really Helena? That is good news, at least that you feel that way. But what can we do about getting released?"

"I suppose I could try to contact my husband," said Helena. "Although I am not really sure that would make any difference."

"Perhaps not, but isn't it worth trying?" replied Annie. "Actually, I have been thinking too. I wonder if Edmund would help me."

"You have spoken little about Edmund, Annie."

"I know because it is too painful. I am regretting turning him down when he proposed."

Helena smiled gently.

"He actually proposed?"

"Well, yes, but at that time, I was convinced that I was going to become a nun. I almost feel like I have been duped into that belief. The priest had such a convincing manner and kept assuring me that I owed God my service. I felt so confused. But now that I have had time to think and my mind is clearer, my desire to have a family has been rekindled. It was all I ever wanted after my mother and sister both died. When my half-sister Rosa was born, although I was very young, I wondered what it would be like if I could have her for my own. I needed someone to love unconditionally. It all seems so foolish now. When I was growing up, all I ever wanted was to find a handsome husband and have a family of my own. When I was forced to look after my siblings, I felt trapped. But I loved them all so much and used to wonder how it would be to have children of my own."

"Where is this Edmund? Perhaps he would forgive you if you let him."

"I don't really know. Perhaps. Do you think I should try contacting him?"

"You should take your own advice, Annie. Isn't it worth trying?" I think it is time that you wrote to Edmund and told him of your change of heart. It may please him to renew your acquaintance. And it sounds like he was very keen on you."

"Do you really think so, Helena?"

"Yes, I do. You must write to him as soon as possible. You must let him know that you have overcome the powerful feelings that were shaping your life and that now your mind is clear and you no longer believe that you should become a nun."

Annie wrote the letter and gave it to the attendants. She felt it was her last hope. That night she knelt by her bed for a long time, saying a silent rosary and pleading with God that Edmund would receive her letter and find a way to help her.

Some days in the asylum were better than others. Work in the laundry and garden stopped on Sundays. Although Annie loved her work in the garden, she was always glad of a break from the drudgery of the laundry.

Annie still attended the church services each Sunday morning, but her obsession with religion was abating. Why would a merciful God have kept her incarcerated in this place for so long? If she was being called to serve God, someone would have rescued her from this place by now.

After the service, the women would spend the rest of the day in the yards. But today the attendants had assembled a group of them, including Annie and Helena, near the front gate.

Matron Lansdowne appeared in the yard, which was a surprise to Annie and the other women. They were not accustomed to seeing her on a Sunday.

"As you have been well behaved this week, you will be allowed to go on an excursion," announced Matron Lansdowne. "You will be going down to the river for a picnic. It is quite a long walk, so those of you who don't feel up to walking should say so now. But otherwise, collect the baskets of food that have been prepared for your lunch and we will begin."

The women looked at each other in astonishment. They had heard that others had been allowed to leave the grounds for brief excursions, but this was the first time any of them had ventured outside the great gates since they had arrived.

Helena and Annie took a basket of food between them and so all the women, including Matron Lansdowne and several of the other attendants, ventured out past the gatehouse and through the gates. It was a pleasant September day and the days were lengthening. Spring was in the air, with the sun shining brightly in the cloudless sky. The improved weather lifted Annie's spirits, but so too did the chance to wander down towards the river.

As they left the asylum behind them, the scent of the gums filled the air as they approached the natural bushland near the river. Spring rains had fallen, bringing the cold winter earth back to life, and wildflowers were popping their heads up through the fresh shoots of green that carpeted the ground. It felt altogether different from walking in the gardens of the asylum. Beautiful as they were, they felt nothing like the bush. Annie longed for the bush, for her country home. She would never enjoy city life.

"Oh Helena, I really must get out of here," she said. "This is not where I belong. I need to return to the country. If only Edmund would write. It has been some time since I wrote to him and still I have heard nothing. If he still cared about me, you would think I would have heard from him by now."

"I know, Annie," said Helena. "The waiting is hard. But I must tell you, I have heard from my husband. I am hopeful that he may relent and get me released."

Annie stared at Helena in disbelief.

"What? You have heard from him?"

"Well, not exactly, but you know that Matron Lansdowne called me to her office yesterday. She told me he had been to see her and asked whether she considered I was fully recovered. She said that she thought he was considering having me released."

"Oh, Helena, I hope it can be true," said Annie. "Do you believe it? Do you really think you might get out of here?"

"I don't know. I won't be getting my hopes up. As much as I want to get out, I also don't know how I can just forgive him and continue our lives as if nothing has happened."

Annie nodded. She understood what Helena was feeling and wondered whether she herself could return to her father's home after he had let her down so dreadfully.

Annie and Helena were thoughtful as they continued to walk with the other women through the bush towards the river. When they arrived at the banks of the Yarra River, all the women sat down to enjoy the picnic lunch and gaze over the beautiful scene, watching the water flowing quietly by. On the other side of the river, they had a view of the hills off in the distance. They chattered happily and munched on the cold mutton sandwiches and the conversation went quiet as a kookaburra laughed with them from high in a gum tree. The happy sound delighted all the women and soon they were laughing along with the kookaburra.

It was a lovely afternoon. After lunch, they packed up their baskets and wandered along the river bank. The river had many twists and turns and there was a new vista around every corner. Sometimes the banks were high and in other parts they could wander right down to the water's edge. Shrieks filled the quiet air when they all removed their shoes and stockings, hitched up their skirts and waded ankle deep into the icy water.

As the shadows lengthened the attendants, who had also obviously enjoyed the outing, hurried them back to collect their picnic baskets and they all regretfully headed back to the asylum. Seeing the asylum walls from the outside again was a strange experience. They could see other inmates in the yard and it was almost possible to believe that they could easily escape over the wall even though they knew that the wall was ten foot high on the other side.

Annie had been summoned to Matron Lansdowne's office. She was nervous but excited. Perhaps there was some news from home. Annie had felt much calmer lately, and she was sure that Matron Lansdowne must know that she was well enough now to be released.

Annie followed the attendant down through the long passageways, passing through the dormitories and the dayroom before being shown into Matron Lansdowne's office. The attendant knocked quietly at the door.

"Come in," came a voice from inside the room. The matron was seated behind her desk. As Annie entered, she leaned back in her chair and twisted the gold wedding band on her finger.

"Ah Annie, please sit down," said Matron Lansdowne. She dismissed the attendant. "That will be all, thank you."

Annie sat down. "Good morning Matron Lansdowne." By now Annie knew not to ask questions. She needed to show that she was restrained and polite in the presence of staff, especially the matron.

Matron Lansdowne looked unsmilingly at Annie leading her to believe that any news that the matron had must be bad.

"There has been a letter, Annie. Whilst I can't allow you to read the letter, I can tell you its contents."

Annie sat bolt upright and clenched her hands together in her lap in an effort to keep her emotions in check. She said nothing, as she was sure whatever she said would be wrong.

Matron Lansdowne continued.

"The letter is from an Edmund Carter who professes to have a kind regard for you, Annie."

Still Annie could not trust herself to speak.

"In response to your letter, Edmund would like you to know that, whilst he would very much like to help you, it is not within his power to influence either the authorities or your family."

Annie gasped. She felt tears forming, threatening to spill over despite Annie's determination to control her emotions.

"Annie, I am sorry to have to give you this news."

Annie gave way to her tears and sobbed bitterly. Her shoulders shook as she finally surrendered to the agony of not knowing what to do next.

"What am I to do?" said Annie through her tears.

"Annie, your mental state seems much improved and the Doctors are pleased with your progress. You must keep up your recovery. That is your only hope of being released. You may go now."

Annie stared at her. The matron was dismissing her so easily. She was losing all hope that she would ever escape this place. She got unsteadily to her feet and left the room. The attendant was waiting outside the door to take her back to the ward.

Helena looked up as she entered. She had obviously been waiting for Annie to return, and Annie could see the worry in her eyes.

"Annie, what's wrong? What happened?"

"It was a letter from Edmund. But he cannot help. I was not even allowed to read the letter."

"Oh Annie, that is awful. But you mustn't lose hope."

"How can I not?" Annie collapsed on her bed and wept inconsolably.

The long days dragged on. Annie was feeling completely hopeless. Her despondent mood caused her to wonder whether she was spiraling back into her previous disturbed state of mind. But through her despair she eventually noticed that Helena was quieter than usual.

"What's wrong Helena?" asked Annie.

Helena smiled sadly.

"My husband is coming to pick me up tomorrow and take me home."

"You are leaving, getting out of here?"

"Yes, it seems so."

"Oh, Helena, that is wonderful news. You will be free."

"I am not really sure how I feel about it. I am feeling much better than when I came in. Some time away from my life and my husband has certainly helped. I have had time to think about why I got so sad and felt that my life was not worth living. But now I wonder if all my doubts will return when I get out of here."

"I think I understand what you mean, but surely anything is better than being trapped in here? However, I know several of the woman think being in here is a lot better than what they had on the outside. I am going to miss you terribly. What do you think your husband will want from you?"

"That is the part I am most concerned about. Why has he chosen to have me released all of a sudden? I hope he doesn't expect that I can just return to the way we were."

"Perhaps you will just need to be strong and stand up to him so that you can have a peaceful life as well."

"The trouble is that I am beholden to him. I have no other means of support. And as a married woman, I cannot be employed."

"Maybe you could take in some mending. Your needlework is very good."

"Well, we will just have to wait and see," said Helena, and the two women hugged briefly.

The following day, Annie watched as Helena packed her few simple possessions into a small bag. Tears formed in Annie's eyes as Helena hugged her tightly.

"I really am going to miss you, Helena. I don't know what I would have done without your friendship. You will write, won't you?" said Annie.

"Of course. But you must promise me you will be sensible and not do anything to get yourself into trouble. You will never be released if you cannot stay calm and in control."

Annie frowned overwhelmed, once again, by her despair.

"I am not sure if they will ever release me."

"Oh Annie. Please don't give up hope. Promise me you will stay strong."

Annie nodded and tried to smile. She watched tearfully as her friend picked up her bag and left the room. Annie had begged to go out into the yard to see Helena off, but she had not been allowed. So, as the door closed behind Helena, she wondered if she would ever see her again.

Chapter Nineteen

Losing Helena's friendship and company weighed heavily on Annie. Whilst she had made other friends, Helena was her closest. She tried to talk to Mabel, but Mabel had very little sympathy for Annie. She was so desperate to stay in the asylum that she could not understand fully how Annie could be so determined to leave.

As Annie's desperation increased, she wondered whether she could escape. She knew others had done so. If she could just get out and into the nearby township of Kew, she felt sure that she would be able to find someone who would help her get back to her family. Although she had not heard from them, and Edmund seemed powerless to help, she longed to go home and reconcile with her family.

Then, suddenly an opportunity presented itself. She was taking a load of freshly laundered sheets to the storage area when she noticed that the door to the main administration area was open ever so slightly. She looked around her. No one seemed to be around. Fear rose in her throat, but she was determined. She quickly deposited the pile of sheets in the cupboard and without pausing to think, moved carefully towards the door. Still no one appeared. Her confidence grew, and she peered through the crack in the door. She could see that the clerk was busy, her head down behind her desk. Annie gently inched the door open just enough to squeeze through. She waited for another minute, then summoned up her courage and quickly and silently ducked past the reception desk and out the open front door.

As soon as she cleared the building, she started to run. She ran as fast as her legs would carry her towards the front gate.

"Hey, stop!" The shout rang out behind Annie.

Her heart skipped a beat, but she continued to run. Her heart was thundering against her ribs. Behind her, she could hear the clerk calling for the attendants.

When Annie reached the front gate, she tried in vain to get the big iron gates open. But they would not budge. Of course they were locked as she should have known they would be if she had been thinking clearly. By this time, the commotion had alerted the gatekeeper and he came out from the gatehouse. He grabbed Annie and tried to restrain her but Annie twisted out of his grip and continued to struggle with the gate. By now, two female attendants and a male attendant had arrived on the scene. Between the four of them they restrained Annie, who was now struggling violently seeming to have called on some super strength from deep within.

They dragged Annie kicking and screaming back into the building where the Doctor was waiting with a syringe to sedate her. When Annie awoke some time later, she once again found herself in an isolation cell. She wept bitterly. But soon her temper got the better of her and she yelled loudly.

"Let me out. You can't keep me in here again. Please don't lock me in here again."

The Doctor was soon summoned, and once again he sedated her.

The next time she came to, there were two attendants watching over her.

"Call Matron Lansdowne," said one of them. The other attendant left the room and soon returned with Matron Lansdowne.

Annie felt groggy and could not understand what was happening to her.

"Annie, what were you thinking?" asked Matron Lansdowne.

"I have to get out of here. I should not be here." Annie had spoken these words many times since she had first arrived. Elsie looked at her with pity.

"I am sorry Annie, but attempting to escape is certainly not the answer. Now you will have to stay in isolation until the Doctor is sure that you won't attempt such a silly thing again."

Annie began to sob again.

"Oh please, Matron Lansdowne. Please don't make me stay here again."

"I have no choice, Annie, but you do. You will need to remain calm and be sensible if you want to return to the ward."

"But I feel so hopeless. No one wants to help me."

"I know it feels that way Annie, but we are all here to help you. And not just those of us inside these walls. I don't know if you are aware but there is a strong movement working for women's rights. I have attended many meetings over the last few years and there is hope that conditions for women will improve. But we women must do more to help ourselves. You must do more to help yourself. Be sensible, please, and then we can get you back to the ward as soon as possible."

Elsie left Annie's cell and closed the door behind her. She could see the scorn in the eyes of the attendants who accompanied her. She knew that the way she sympathised with Annie and some of the other inmates did not impress them. They obviously just thought of Annie simply as a troublemaker. But Elsie did not care. She had to find a way to help Annie because, despite the trouble she had been in, Elsie agreed that the young girl should not be locked away any longer. Elsie recognised that Annie was an intelligent young woman who had just acted unwisely and impetuously. When she had first been admitted, she had definitely been disturbed, what with her ranting and raving about needing to devote her life to God one minute and the next saying she wanted nothing more than to marry her beau and have a family of her own. But she had certainly recovered and staying here was not helping her mental state.

Annie felt completely desolate having found herself back in the isolation ward. Her body was racked with sobs and her face was streaked with tears.

The medication was taking effect, and the familiar fog descended on her brain. Through her addled thoughts, one thing kept surfacing. She needed to get out of here. Out of this dreaded isolation ward, out of the asylum.

Despite the power of the drugs coursing through her veins, she paced the room. It was so unfair. She should never have been here in the first place. Eventually, though, she collapsed onto the narrow mattress on the floor of the tiny cell, completely exhausted by her anguish and her temper and overcome by the drugs, she fell into a disturbed sleep.

When she awoke some hours later, it was early morning, and her head had cleared slightly. It took a moment for her to realise where she was as she looked around in horror. Again, she was locked away on her own. She had no idea how long she had spent in isolation last time and the thought of having to endure any amount of time on her own again made her sob uncontrollably yet again. She cast her mind back to all that had happened to her since she had been here.

She knew all too well from previous experience that she needed to remain calm in order to be released from this cell. It would take all her resolve. She must be strong and she must try to refuse the drugs. Although they numbed her mind and helped her to forget the situation she was in, she remembered all too well how distressing it was for the first few weeks, when they were no longer given to her. She did not want to have to go through that again. She knew someone would be here soon with her breakfast and the Doctor would probably be there also to administer the injection that she longed for but knew she must avoid at all costs.

She heard the door being opened. She strengthened her resolve and dried her tears. Sheila opened the door. Annie cringed. Sheila grinned spitefully.

"Well, who do we have here? I should have known you would soon find your way back here. You are a wicked girl, Annie. This is the best place for you."

Annie could not believe her bad luck. Of all the attendants, Sheila was the last person she had hoped to see this morning. She drew in a deep breath and attempted a smile.

"Hello Sheila, yes, I am back in here. But I don't intend it to be for long."

"We will see about that." Sheila left her breakfast by the door and was about to close it when the Doctor arrived.

"Good morning Annie. How are you this morning?"

Despite her shock at seeing Sheila, Annie kept control and spoke politely to the Doctor.

"Good morning Doctor. I am quite well, thank you. Do you really think I need to be in isolation?"

"Well Annie, you were very foolish yesterday, trying to run away. We will need to keep you here until we can be sure that you won't try to escape again."

"Yes, I know how foolish that was, Doctor, and I would never attempt it again. I don't know what made me think I could just run away."

"Anyway, I am a busy man. Give me your arm."

"Please Doctor, I really don't think that I need to be sedated. You can see that I am completely calm and rational."

"I am sorry Annie, I can't take a chance on you hurting yourself or anyone else."

He took her arm and gave her the injection. Despite not wanting the drugs, Annie remained calm. The fog descended on her brain again as Sheila and the Doctor left the tiny cell.

The days went by slowly, and each day Annie tried to refuse the drugs. After the third or fourth day, Annie wasn't sure which, as her mind was becoming dull again the Doctor apparently decided that she did not need the drugs and left without administering an injection. Annie was euphoric. She could hardly believe that she had managed to keep her wits about her and remain calm enough that she had convinced the Doctor that she did not need to be sedated. She was learning. This was the only way they would ever release her from this place. She must control her emotions and not let her anger get the better of her.

A few days later, her euphoria increased. The door opened and the matron entered.

"Oh, Matron Lansdowne, it is so good to see you." The matron smiled at Annie. She had had excellent reports of Annie's behaviour.

"It is good to see you looking so well to Annie. It seems you are beginning to understand that you must keep control of your emotions if you are ever to be released."

"Is there a chance I can at least go back to the ward?"

"That is why I am here. I came to see if all the reports I have been receiving are true. And it looks to me as if you are ready to go back to the ward and to your work. The garden is missing you. But you must promise me you will never try that silly stunt of trying to escape again."

"It was so foolish of me, Matron Lansdowne. I know I would never have really been able to escape. I certainly would not be foolish enough to try again."

"Very well. The final decision will be up to the Doctor, but I think you will soon be able to be released from isolation."

"Thank you. I won't disappoint you."

Chapter Twenty

E lsie sat in her office, wishing the day would end. She had been feeling quite hopeless of late. Whilst she had always believed in the benefits of the treatments offered here, she realised that not all the women reacted well. There seemed little she could do to help any of the women in her charge. She had often tried to let her opinions be known to the doctors and the superintendent but her words fell on deaf ears. They seemed to think that her opinion was not worth considering. As a qualified nurse, she felt that her opinion should garner more respect. The frustration got to her at times and this was one of these times. It was her day off tomorrow and she could not wait to get away tonight and spend some time at home where she lately felt so safe and content.

There was a knock at the door, and one of the clerks entered.

"What is it?" she asked.

"There is a young man here who says he is a friend of Annie Moore and that he would like to see her. I have told him that is not possible, but he is very persistent."

Elsie thought for a moment. She thought it would probably not be wise to allow Annie to have a visitor so soon after her release from the refractory ward. But Elsie was curious, so she agreed to see him.

"Show him in, please."

The clerk left the room and returned a few minutes later with a good-looking young man.

"Matron Lansdowne, this is Edmund Carter, who has come to enquire about Annie."

"Thank you. Please take a seat, Mr Carter. My name is Matron Lansdowne."

"Good morning Matron Lansdowne," said Edmund. "My name is Edmund Carter and I insist on seeing Annie Moore."

Elsie straightened her back and put on her severest look. Although she was pleased to see the young man who might be able to help Annie, she could not allow him to think he could put any pressure on her. She must do what was best for the inmates.

"I am sorry, young man, but there is little point coming in here and making demands. It will not advance your cause. Please take a seat."

Edmund slumped into a chair and Elsie could see that his bluster was not his usual way and the wind was taken out of his sails.

"I am sorry, Matron. It is just that I am so worried about Annie. I left her at a boarding house when she wouldn't return to her father's home. She was very upset. I should have done more to help her. When I went back the next morning she was

gone. I tried to find her. Her family didn't know where she
was. Her father was angry and said she was a grown woman
and would just have to look after herself. But I kept trying to
find her. I was completely shocked when I received her letter. I
cannot tell you. There has been some mistake. I simply cannot
believe that she is mad. Why has she not been allowed to leave?
When I wrote back I really thought there was nothing I could
do to help Annie. But I am really very fond of her. There must
be something I can do."

Elsie was unsure how much she should tell this young man.
She decided she needed to try to reassure him.

"I can tell you that Annie is much better at the moment. She
has had a trying time but is recovering well."

The relief was clear on Edmund's face.

"Does that mean you will release her soon?"

"I am sorry. I did not mean to mislead you. It is not my
decision. I do not have the authority to decide when, or indeed
if, Annie should be released. To this point, there has been no
one to vouch for her safety should she be released."

"I will vouch for her."

"But you are not a relative, are you?"

Edmund looked crestfallen.

"No, I am not, but I am deeply concerned for her."

"I am sorry. There is nothing I can do unless her next of kin
makes an application on her behalf."

"Can I see her?"

"That is really not possible at the moment, young man. Visitors are only allowed under extreme circumstances."

"What can I do to help her?"

"As I said, the only thing that would help is if her father applied to have her released. Do you have a relationship with him? Perhaps you could convince him to have Annie released."

Edmund seemed relieved that there was some course of action he could take.

"I have worked with Mr Moore. He is a good man. I will go to see him immediately. I only hope he will listen to me. Thank you, Matron Lansdowne. Please give Annie my regards."

"That I can do," said Elsie, allowing herself a small smile.

Edmund stood up and, with a nod to Elsie, left the room and was escorted to the entrance hall by the clerk.

Elsie sighed. He seemed like such a nice young man, despite his bluster at the beginning of their meeting. She hoped that he would have some sway with Annie's father, although she was not entirely convinced that his word would count for anything. But perhaps there was some hope for Annie. Poor Annie. She wished there was more she could do to help the hapless young woman.

Annie returned to the dormitory. She felt strong and calm and was proud of herself because she had managed to remain so through her time in isolation. She knew she was truly well enough to be released and go back to her family. Although she had had no contact with them, she longed to be reunited with her father. And Rosa. She had missed the pretty little girl who had come to depend on her so much. Annie wondered what it would be like to see her half sister again after so many months. Would Rosa still look up to her, or would she be afraid of Annie's illness? Perhaps Rosa would hate her for leaving all the children alone without her help.

Mabel was pleased to see Annie when she returned to the dormitory. Both girls extended their arms and embraced each other. It was a bright sunny spring morning, so the two girls made their way out to the yard with the other women and were soon strolling around the bright spring garden.

"I am so glad you are back, Annie. I missed you," said Mabel. "What on earth happened? Someone said you tried to escape."

Annie related her attempted escape to the astonished Mabel.

"Oh Annie, what were you thinking? You must have known you would never actually be able to escape. Even if you got past the gates, they would soon have found you and brought you back."

"Yes, I know, it was a foolish thing to do, but I just saw the open door and didn't really think at all."

The sun felt warm on Annie's skin while the breeze brushed her curls, bouncing her hair, which had once again escaped its pins, against her cheeks. The magpies were chortling in the gum trees and soon they would be darting. Anyone who ventured too close as they protected their young in their nests would feel their wrath. The garden was just coming into bloom and within days it would be a riot of colour. Butterflies shimmered in the sunlight as they fluttered from flower to flower. The scent of spring and new life filled the air.

"Spring gives me such hope, Mabel," said Annie. "Perhaps my father will come for me now."

"What makes you think that? So far, he seems to have ignored your plight in here." Mabel was much recovered after her recent malaise but still had a rather jaundiced view of the outside world.

"I know, but I have a good feeling. And I am truly well now. I no longer have any confusion about what I want to do with my life. I really would like to marry. If only Edmund will still have me. I hurt him so dreadfully, I would not be surprised if he could not forgive me." Despite her current good spirits, Annie sighed at this thought.

An attendant suddenly appeared next to the pair.

"Come Annie, Matron Lansdowne wishes to speak to you."

Annie looked at Mabel and smiled. The look said everything. Annie felt hopeful that there would be good news and Mabel returned the smile. Annie followed the attendant into the building and knocked at Matron Lansdowne's office door.

"Come in," came the familiar voice from inside. Annie opened the door and entered.

"There you are Annie, please sit down. I have news."

Annie did as she was asked and sat down in the hard wooden chair. She remained silent. She had learned that silence was an excellent strategy.

"I have had a visit from Edmund Carter." Annie chewed her lip but still said nothing.

"He seems a very respectable young man, and he is very fond of you. He really wants to help."

Finally, Annie could restrain herself no longer. Against her better judgement, she sat forward in her chair and spoke out loudly.

"Edmund was here? Why wasn't I allowed to see him? You are cruel Matron Lansdowne."

"Annie." Matron Lansdowne's tone was stern. Annie immediately sat back in her chair and took a deep breath.

"I am sorry, Matron Lansdowne. It is just that I miss Edmund terribly. In fact, I miss everyone. I have only had one letter from my sister Rosa. I miss them all."

Matron Lansdowne's face softened. She was pleased to hear that Annie still had feelings for Edmund. He seemed a decent man and even though Elsie did not necessarily believe marriage was the best course of action for every woman, she felt that Annie could do a lot worse than to marry him.

"I know Annie. But I did not think it prudent to allow you to visit with the young man until we are more certain about your future. I have informed him that there is little he can do to have you released, other than to convince your father to petition for your release. So that is what he proposed to do when he left here.

So, if your health continues to improve and you remain under control, there may be some small hope of your release."

Annie could barely believe her ears. Edmund was going to see her father. It was wonderful news. But Annie knew that Matron Lansdowne was right. She really had every reason now to be on her best behavior. There might be genuine hope again. Her father might come for her.

Annie and Mabel had become even closer since Helena had been released. They still worked together in the laundry, and they were seldom apart when they had any free time.

Annie had been encouraging Mabel to learn to read. Mabel had not had a lot of schooling and struggled to read the books that were available. Annie would often read aloud to her and then encourage Mabel to read short passages too.

When there were newspapers available, which certainly was not a regular occurrence, Annie would pour over them, hungry for any news of the outside world.

"Listen to this Mabel," said Annie as the two women sat leafing through the papers that had just arrived in the ward.

WOMEN'S SUFFRAGE. 15th October 1894

A meeting, under the chairmanship of Mr. R. W. Best, M.L. A., was held in the Fitzroy town hall on Thursday evening to form a branch of the Victorian Women's Franchise League. Addresses were delivered by Mrs. Besant Scott, Rev. J. Hoatson, of New

Zealand, and Crs. Millis and McMahon, and it was unanimously decided that a branch of the league be at once formed. At the termination of the address, a large number of members, both ladies and gentlemen, were enrolled.

"What do you think about that Mabel?" asked Annie. She knew Mabel was a strong and opinionated young girl, so she was interested in hearing what she thought.

"I am sure I don't know, Annie. I don't really understand much about women's suffrage."

Annie thought for a moment. Of course, Mabel would not know much about how hard women were working to get the vote. So she proceeded to explain.

"Women are fighting for the equal right to vote. Matron Lansdowne told me that she is involved with the local women's suffrage movement. Apparently this group has been formed to advance the rights of Victorian women. Personally, I just want to marry and have a family, so I have little interest in whether or not I can vote. I will be quite happy to allow my husband to make the decisions."

"Oh my word, Annie. I can't believe I am hearing this. A strong woman like you. Surely you would like to have some say in how you live your life? After all, it is because men have all the power that you are locked up in here. Maybe if women had more rights, I would have been able to get a proper job and not have had to resort to being a lady of the night."

Annie felt suitably chastened.

"You are right, of course, Mabel." She went back to reading the paper, vowing to give the matter much more thought.

Branches of the Victorian Women's Franchise League were springing up all over Melbourne. Elsie had continued the fight. Three years had passed since the monster petition had been tabled in parliament and still there seemed little progress. It was a great source of frustration that even though the gathering of signatures had resulted in a bill being tabled for women's franchise the Legislative Council had failed to pass the bill.

Elsie was in the city to attend a meeting. There seemed new hope. Annette Bear had instigated the United Council for Women's Suffrage and had been elected President of the new group just this year. Annette had already addressed today's crowd. Now there was a determined newcomer on the scene. Elsie had met Vida Goldstein at earlier meetings, but under Annette's mentorship she was becoming very outspoken for women's rights. Vida addressed the meeting for the first time.

"Ladies, the main purpose of this new organisation is, as the name suggests, to lobby the Victorian Government to grant franchise to women. We must have a vote in order to take control of our lives."

Annette was soon to be married to a wonderful and supportive man, William Crawford. He was a solicitor and also believed in women having the vote. Elsie had been invited to the wedding, an event she was very much looking forward to. But she couldn't help but wonder if Annette would still be so active in the movement following her wedding. Perhaps Vida Goldstein would now play a bigger role.

The only letter Annie had received since she had been locked away was the letter from Rosa. That seemed so long ago. She still had the precious letter carefully hidden in her bag. Often, when no one was around, she would get it out and read it. She knew all the words by heart. She knew too that Edmund had also written to her, but the matron had not allowed her to read that letter. So she was stunned when she was handed another letter. The envelope had been opened, so she knew that it had been read before she had been allowed to see it. Even so, it was such a wonderful thing to hold the letter, which would surely contain some news of the outside world.

She looked at the envelope and turned it over slowly to see the name and address of the sender. It was from Helena. She had been Annie's saviour. If it wasn't for her friendship, Annie did not know where she would be. She missed her dreadfully. Annie had tears in her eyes as she turned the letter over and over, afraid to read it. What if the reconciliation with her husband had not gone well?

Her desire to read Helena's words eventually overrode her fears that the letter would contain bad news. With shaking hands, she withdrew the paper from the envelope.

24th October 1894

Dearest Annie,

I hope this finds you well. I have not stopped thinking about you. How have you been? I do hope that your release is imminent.

I am well and quite happy. My husband has been kind since my release. We are living in a small cottage, which we rent from a cranky landlord. But it is all we need and is close to the river bank, so we have a lovely outlook. My husband has a good job and is working hard and we are getting along very well.

Please write back if you can. I long to know that you are in good spirits.

Your friend always,

Helena.

Tears fell onto the paper, making tiny smudges on the ink. She held the letter up to her nose, sensing that there was a faint scent of Helena on the paper. Annie was so happy for her friend and pleased that everything had worked out so well. Now if only she could get out of this place herself. The letter from Helena had given her hope that one day her life might be blissful too. Surely the letter was a good omen.

Chapter Twenty-One

E lsie knew it was time to act. She had given a great deal of thought to her meeting with Edmund, Annie's handsome young friend. He seemed very concerned about her wellbeing so she hoped he had been able to talk to Annie's father. It was obvious to Elsie that Annie needed to be released, but what could she do? She felt the heavy weight of responsibility on her shoulders. She needed to do more.

Strengthening her resolve, she rose from her desk and, with a determined step, headed for Doctor Woodforde's office. She knocked firmly on the door.

"Who is it?" came the deep voice.

Elsie opened the door a crack and announced herself.

"What do you want? Come in, come in," he said impatiently.

Elsie entered the room and without being invited, took a seat opposite the desk, trying to show confidence that she did not feel.

Doctor Woodforde did not raise his eyes from his work.

"Well, what can I do for you?"

Elsie was silent for a moment before she spoke in a clear, even tone.

"It is about one of the inmates, Annie Moore. I consider her to be well enough to be released."

Doctor Woodforde's head jerked up from his paperwork, and he raised his monocle to his eye and gave Elsie a stunned look. It was obvious to Elsie that he was nonplussed at her taking the liberty of speaking out.

"Excuse me? So you are telling me you think someone is ready for release? Under what authority?"

Elsie sat up very straight in her chair. Despite the Doctor's withering look she was determined to continue.

"I am a qualified nurse and have been working with these women for years now. I think I have some credibility to be able to assess whether or not they are recovering."

"Is that so?" Elsie noticed a small grin on his dour features. Surely, he was not amused by her suggestion?

He continued. "Matron Lansdowne, I appreciate you are very caring towards these women, but I think you should leave the medical diagnoses to those who are imminently more qualified than yourself."

Elsie could see that he placed absolutely no store in her opinion but she was determined to persist.

"Yes, doctor, I do care for all the women, which is why I feel I know them quite well."

"I do not need your opinion, Matron, and actually in this case, I do not agree with you. I know the patient to whom you refer, and I think she needs more time with us."

Elsie was fuming. She had known before she entered his office that her opinion would count for little but could not believe she was being dismissed so easily. But it would not do Annie's cause any good to lose her temper now. She was already wondering if her interference had done Annie more harm than good. Once again, she took a deep breath to control her rioting emotions and straightened her back in the chair.

"I understand, doctor, but all I am asking is that you check on Annie. I am sure you must see that she is much improved."

The doctor looked at Elsie.

"That will be all, Matron Lansdowne." He went back to his paperwork and Elsie knew it was futile to say anything further, so she got up and left the room. Once outside, she leant against the wall, squeezing her eyes shut against the tears of anger that threatened to overtake her. All she could hope was that the Doctor might take a little more notice of Annie's condition next time he was called on to examine her. It was little enough, but it was all that Elsie could do.

Elsie was still seething when she returned to the office. She sat down and reached for the record book, trying to compose herself to continue her notes, but it was hard to block out her confrontation with Doctor Woodforde from her mind. It had been bad enough having her own opinion discounted, but knowing there was really nothing she could do for Annie was just too much to bear. She sighed and consoled herself with the thought that at least she had tried.

Days passed and still Elsie seemed unable to do anything to advance Annie's case for release. She had heard nothing further from Edmund or from Annie's father. All she could really do was hope that Edmund had taken her advice and gone to Annie's father to help him understand that she needed him to advocate for her release.

It surprised her when one morning Doctor Woodforde summoned her to his office. *What can he possibly want?* she thought. *He has little regard for my opinion, so he can't be wanting to talk to me about the inmates.* With this thought running through her mind, she made her way to his office.

He answered her knock at the door and she entered.

"Please sit down, Matron Lansdowne."

Elsie sat down but pulled herself up to her full height, wanting to appear strong and unphased by his obvious contempt for her. Her gaze was unwavering.

"How can I help you, Doctor Woodforde?"

"It seems your little project to look after Annie Moore may have had some impact. I received a letter from her father and he is interested in having her released."

Elsie could not contain her pleasure.

"That is excellent news, doctor. When can she be released?"

"Now let's not be too hasty, Matron Lansdowne. We must take this slowly. We cannot just release her based on a request. I will need to ensure she is well enough to be released into the community. We have a responsibility to ensure that anyone who is released will not be a danger to themselves or to others."

Elsie thought it would be in Annie's best interest if she were to side with the doctor.

"Of course, Doctor Woodforde. Are you able to make time to make that assessment soon?"

Doctor Woodforde looked thoughtful and was silent for a long minute. Elsie held her breath.

"I think perhaps that would be wise. Overcrowding is becoming an increasingly large problem, so if there is anyone who can be released, then we should act as quickly as possible. Please bring Annie to me straight away."

Elsie was elated. She left immediately to find Annie. It was a fine day and most of the inmates were in the yard, taking part in their exercise. Elsie sought out Annie and told her that the doctor wanted to see her.

Annie swallowed hard. Her hand flew to her hair, tucking stray strands behind her ears.

"What does he want?" she asked.

Elsie did not want to get Annie's hopes up. She was likely to spiral into despair if things did not go well.

"Just follow me please, Annie."

The two women entered the building and proceeded down the long hallway to Doctor Woodforde's office. Elsie waited outside the office when Annie was called in.

"Please come in and sit down," said Doctor Woodforde. "How have you been feeling?"

Annie sat on the edge of the chair wondering what this was about.

"I am feeling quite well, thank you doctor."

"I can see that you have colour in your cheeks and your eyes are bright. Have you been having any bad dreams or any fits of anger or otherwise?"

"No sir, I have felt very calm of late. In fact, I feel much recovered and I don't think I need to be here any longer."

"Hmm, you must let me be the judge of that. But yes, you seem to be quite well at the moment, Annie. I have some news. I have received a letter from your father."

Annie gasped, but otherwise remained silent. She did not trust herself to speak.

"It appears that he would petition for your release. As you may or may not be aware, we would need him to sign your release papers and we would need to return you to his authority."

Annie still did not trust herself to speak. She looked at the doctor hopefully.

"Well, what have you got to say for yourself, young lady?"

There was a tremor in Annie's voice as she finally managed to get the words out.

"I can't quite believe that after all this time there may be a chance that I can go home. But I am well enough. I know I am well enough."

"Very well, then I will write back to your father and get the paperwork started."

Annie was lightheaded and as she got to her feet to leave the office, she felt she might faint. She could not believe what she was hearing. Did this really mean that they would finally release her?

Annie paced nervously in the dayroom. Finally she sat down on the edge of a chair next to Mabel. She noticed the concerned look on Mabel's face.

"What is it Annie?" enquired her friend.

"My father has finally come. I will be called to see him soon." She was struggling to believe that after all this time, he had finally come. Could it really be true? What would she say to him? Her anger had passed long ago, but now she just wondered if she would ever be able to rebuild her relationship with her father. She loved him, as always, and wanted more than anything to be able to forgive him. But she was really not sure that she could. She could not delay any longer.

She rose from the chair where she had been sitting waiting to be called to the matron's office. Had she slept in this horrid place for the last time? There was one last hurdle to scale before they finally released her. She must meet with her father and assure him she was well enough and would not be any trouble if he signed the papers for her release.

Now the attendant was waiting impatiently to show her to the Matron's office where her father waited. She walked slowly behind the attendant.

"Do hurry Annie, I haven't got all day."

Eventually they stood outside the office. Annie's hands shook as the attendant knocked at the door.

The door opened and there he was. Annie saw her father for the first time in eight long months. He looked exactly as she remembered, which seemed strange to Annie. It felt like an eternity since she had seen him last. So much had happened. Somehow, she had expected him to look different.

The matron was seated behind her desk and Doctor Woodforde stood to the side, looking sternly at Annie, his monocle to his eye.

Frederick rose slowly from his chair as Annie entered the room.

"Annie, it is good to see you."

"It is good to see you too, father." She wanted desperately to talk privately with him. She had so many questions. But she wasn't sure she could control her emotions to talk candidly to her father, and she was fearful that the doctor would think that she was losing her mind again.

"The family has missed you, Annie, all your sisters and brothers and your mother."

"I have missed you all too," Annie could feel the tears welling in her eyes. She brushed them away hurriedly.

"Doctor Woodforde tells me you are well enough to come home."

"Yes, I believe I am quite recovered. Thank you." This polite conversation was getting them nowhere.

The doctor had been watching the two of them carefully.

"We will leave you alone for a few minutes to talk. Come Matron."

"How are you really, Annie?" asked her father when the doctor and the matron had left the room.

Annie could contain her grief no longer.

"Where were you, father? Why didn't you come for me?"

Her father looked at her sadly and slumped back into his chair. Annie moved closer and sank heavily into the chair beside him.

"I am sorry Annie. I did not know what to do. When you left, I was angry with you and, to be frank, the house was more peaceful without you. You and your mother had so many cross words."

"You forget, she is not really my mother. I lost my mother years ago." Annie could not contain her bitterness. "Do you know what has happened to me since I have been here? I have been restrained and put in isolation. They have given me drugs, which made me dull and stupid. I have even had cold water treatment, which is torture, although it is supposed to be calming."

The words tripped and fell out of Annie. She had restrained herself for so long. And now she had to vent, and she felt her father deserved to know all the bad things that had happened to her because he had abandoned her.

Her father's face crumpled. Annie could see that her words had wounded him deeply and suddenly she felt sorry for him.

"Oh father, I am sorry. I really don't want to hurt you, but it has been a living nightmare, and you are supposed to protect me."

"I know Annie. I have let you down. But now I sincerely want to make up for what has happened. Your stepmother cares for you Annie. She wants you to come home."

"I am sure she does, so that I can go back to being her slave."

"No, that is not true, Annie. She was very upset when you left. She understands why you were so determined to run away because she pushed you too hard. When you come home, you will be free to choose your own way."

At that moment, the doctor and the matron returned to the room. Doctor Woodforde regarded them thoughtfully before he spoke.

"Thank you, Annie, that will be all. We need to speak to your father now." With that Annie was ushered out of the office and led back to the day room. But it was not long before the matron once again appeared looking for Annie. She smiled broadly as she ushered Annie out into the corridor.

"It is good news Annie," said the matron. "Your father has signed the release papers and you are free to leave."

"Really? I can't believe it, Matron. I can't thank you enough for all you have done."

"I am just so pleased that I have been able to do something to help you. I know you will bloom once you get back to your beloved hometown."

Annie was not sure how she felt as she entered the office again.

"Annie, we have assessed your case and we believe you are indeed well enough to be released," said the doctor. "You should go and pack your things and you can leave now with your father."

Annie could not believe her ears.

"Now? Today?"

"Yes, hurry now. Your father does not have all day to wait for you."

Annie looked at her father questioningly. Did he really want her to come home with him? The look of tenderness on his face convinced her he was indeed sorry and wanted to atone for his actions. She hurried from the office. Not that there was much to pack up. Her belongings were few. However, she must find Mabel and her other friends to say goodbye.

She went back to the dayroom and Mabel and the other women looked at her questioningly.

"I am being released."

"Really Annie?" exclaimed Mabel. "When will you be leaving?"

"Immediately, as soon as I pack my things."

Mabel pulled Annie into a firm hug as the others watched on in astonishment. It was a rare thing to see someone leave.

"Annie, that is wonderful news," said Mabel. "I know how much you wanted this. Come, let me help you pack."

The two girls went arm in arm into the dormitory. The attendant came in carrying the clothing and other belongings that had been stored since the day she was admitted. As she slowly removed the heavy dress she had worn every day of her incarceration and put on her own clothes, she felt a weight lift off her. Mabel pulled her bag out from under the bed and helped her to pack her things, including her precious prayer book and rosary beads.

"Oh Mabel," said Annie. "I will miss you dreadfully."

"And I will miss you too, Annie. But you know this place is now my home. I have nowhere else that I would rather be. But you, you have a big wonderful family who loves you. And you have Edmund. Now you can make it up with him. Perhaps he will propose again."

Annie blushed. She now recognised that she had deep feelings for Edmund and she could barely contain her excitement at the thought of seeing him again. But she was worried about what he would think of her now. After all, she had been in a mental asylum. Would he consider that she was completely recovered, or would he think of her as damaged goods?

She picked up her bag, and the two girls hugged again. Both had tears streaming down their faces as Annie turned to follow the attendant down the long corridor one last time. As she left, Annie glanced over her shoulder and gave Mabel a bright smile.

The dayroom was crowded and noisy as usual. As Annie passed through she saw Sheila dealing with a poor woman who had just vomited all over her. She would certainly not miss the cruelty meted out by attendants such as Sheila. But Annie was leaving and she knew that whilst Sheila was not locked away, she really had no more escape than any of the other women from the horror of the asylum.

She called her goodbyes to all the other women as she went through the dayroom and soon she was back at the matron's office.

"Everything is in place Annie," said Matron Lansdowne. "You are free to go." Annie had waited so long to hear those words and now she stood stock still, frozen to the spot, wondering if her feet would carry her out of this place.

"I don't know how to thank you Matron," said Annie. "I know you always had my best interests at heart and did everything you could to help me."

"Of course, Annie. It is my job to ensure that the care given here is of the highest possible standard. I try to help all the women."

Annie reached out with both arms to hug the matron. Although Elsie looked rather startled, after a moment she returned the hug.

As Annie and her father made their way out of the building and approached the gatehouse, she half expected someone to call out for her to stop and to tell her that there had been a mistake.

But the gate opened and she and her father stepped through. She looked over her shoulder one last time. At last she was free. Eight long months had passed, but to Annie, it seemed like a lifetime.

As Elsie watched father and daughter leave together, she wondered how it had come to this. Annie and her father obviously had a fractured relationship but underneath it, Elsie felt a definite current of love between them. Why had they grown so far apart? She was convinced that now that Annie was completely recovered from her bout of mania, they would be able to repair their relationship.

Doctor Woodforde turned to Elsie with a smug look.

"That was a good result, Matron. Wouldn't you agree?"

Despite her happiness at seeing Annie reunited with her father, Elsie's anger boiled just below the surface.

"Yes, it is a good result, one which could have been facilitated earlier."

"Don't tell me you are questioning my judgment again Matron?"

Elsie sighed.

"No doctor, but I do think Annie might have been released sooner and perhaps there are others in this institution who don't really need to be here."

"Well, you are entitled to your opinion, Matron. But fortunately I am the doctor here, and I make the decisions."

Elsie pushed down her anger and decided that, for the moment, she would just allow herself a moment to feel proud that, despite everything, she had managed to help secure Annie's freedom. The men in Elsie's life had always stood in her way and that was not about to change anytime soon. But she would continue to work even harder for the rights of the women in her care. She would continue her work towards gaining the vote for women. It had proved a difficult assignment and sometimes she and the other women felt hopeless. But having had this small success with Annie, Elsie felt that change could eventually happen.

Elsie hoped with all her heart that Annie would be able to reconcile with that nice young man and that one day they might be married. She knew that Annie was now strong enough to know her own mind and not be controlled by anyone and she hoped that she would have a happy marriage.

If only Elsie's marriage had not been so unhappy. But she realised she had also developed resilience and courage from all she had been through and had come out of it a much stronger woman. She still grieved for her daughter and wished that they could still be together but right now she felt a sense of contentment and for the moment that would have to do.

Chapter Twenty-Two

F rederick took Annie's bag and placed it in the buggy he had hired in the city and then helped Annie up into the seat. The pair of horses stood patiently, swishing the flies with their tails. The persistent flies settled on their backs again as soon as the horse's tails stilled. Frederick climbed into the buggy and picked up the reins. Soon they were on their way to Spencer Street railway station.

It was a fresh spring day. The Yarra River was flowing swiftly, brimming with water from the freshly melted snow at its source on Mt Baw Baw, as it wound its way to Hobson's Bay. Her father had so far only said a few words, but as the silence lengthened, he obviously felt compelled to speak.

"Annie, I don't know where to start," said Frederick. "So much has happened since you have been away. For a start, we have moved back to Avoca. The gold is running out at the Grand Duke mine. So I decided that the best course of action was to reopen the butcher shop. I have had to take on other work carting and there is not a lot of money, but we are managing."

"That is indeed good news, father," said Annie. What she really wanted to talk about was why he had left her for so long, but her father seemed determined to avoid that subject.

"Yes, Annie. I know how much you disliked our living conditions in Timor. Now we are back in our own comfortable home."

"How are the children, father?" asked Annie. "I missed Rosa terribly."

"They are well and growing quickly. Rosa will be very pleased to see you. She was dreadfully upset when you left."

She thought to herself, what did he mean by that? Did he really believe she had any choice other than to leave? It was almost as if he blamed her for Rosa's distress.

Before long they arrived at the railway station. Annie felt overwhelmed by all the noise and activity. She followed her father down the long platform to where the Maryborough train stood belching steam. Soon they had boarded the train and stowed their bags. The whistle sounded as the train pulled out of the station.

Annie was pleased to leave the noise and chaos of the town behind, and it wasn't long before they were in the lonely countryside. She looked out the window at the paddocks covered with daisies and other wildflowers. Sheep grazed lazily, and the kangaroos looked up as the train passed.

The small talk continued on the long journey. They changed trains at Maryborough to continue on to Avoca. They were both exhausted by the time they arrived at the Avoca railway station. Frederick carried Annie's bag on the short walk from the station to their home. Not much had changed in the town of Avoca. The river was high after the heavy winter rains and as they crossed the bridge, Annie caught her first sight of home.

She looked at the beautiful home that she had lived in most of her life but had not seen for over two years. Memories came flooding back. She thought of her mother. Those memories had become vague and Annie thought guiltily that her mother's face had faded in her memory over the fourteen years since her death. She thought too of Cora. Sadness swept over her.

Suddenly, Rosa burst from the house.

"Annie, is it really you?" Annie held out her arms and Rosa ran into her embrace. Annie felt her heart was fit to burst as she pulled back and held her baby sister at arm's length so that she could look at her properly.

"Yes, I am home. And how you have grown."

The other children tumbled out of the house, all talking at once and trying to hug her. Her stepmother appeared and waited patiently for the children to complete their welcome. Annie noticed that her stepmother appeared to be pregnant again. She could not help but feel annoyed at the thought of another child in the already large family.

"Hello Annie, it is good to see you. You are looking so well."

"Hello Mother, it is good to see you too."

It seemed her stepmother did not share Frederick's reticence to talk about the past and she wasted no time apologising to Annie.

"I am so, so sorry, Annie. I had no idea that you were so unhappy."

Annie looked at her stepmother, trying to see whether she really believed her own words. Could her stepmother really not have known how much distress Annie had been going through?

"It is wonderful to be home," Annie answered noncommittally.

Later, after the children were all in bed, Annie sat with her parents in the comfortable sitting room with its plush sofas and velvet drapes. Annie rose from her seat and wandered over to the mantelpiece. She picked up the small portrait of her mother that had sat there ever since her mother's death. When the house had been closed up and some of their possessions had been moved to Timor, this precious portrait had not been among them. Annie had not seen the picture of her mother for several years. The memories came rushing back. It was a relief to see it again and know that whilst memories of her beloved mother had faded, that they could still come back with some prompting. Annie looked around her, trying to reconcile the fact that she was home and that her life could return to normal. It felt so strange to contemplate what had happened over the last year and yet to be so unsure about her future.

"How are you feeling Annie?" asked Frederick.

"Quite honestly, I don't know how I feel, father," she replied.

Lillie looked slightly chastened as she appeared to struggle to know what to say.

"Annie, as I said, I really am very sorry that I have caused you pain. It was definitely not my intention. I am afraid I was so focused on my own problems that I quite forgot that you are a young girl with a life of your own."

"I cannot understand how you could fail to see my unhappiness. I felt like a slave in my own home. From now on, I need to live my own life. I cannot be at your beck and call all the time."

"I know, and I understand that now. Whilst you were away, I came to realise just how much you did when I had to pick up the pieces myself. But we are all coping quite well now. Rosa is such a good girl and helps out with the younger ones."

"I just hope Rosa does not find herself in the same position as I was in and has some freedom to be a child and to have time for herself. She is a talented pianist, you know."

"Oh Annie, I really have learnt my lesson. Rosa will be fine. I am sure you will see when you have been home for a time."

Annie could see her father was becoming uncomfortable with Lillie's frank discussion.

"Perhaps we should change the subject," said Frederick. "We are finally back in our home and I am working very hard to ensure that we have everything we need. I think we can all start over."

Annie looked at her father quizzically, wondering if he thought talk of their problems might upset her too much, perhaps even rekindle her mania. So she left it at that for now.

"Have you seen Edmund, father?" she asked. "He came to visit me, but I was not allowed to see him."

"No, I haven't seen him since we returned to Avoca. But you know Annie, that he came to see me just before we left Timor. He was terribly upset when he received your letter. He implored me to take action to have you released. If it had not been for him, I don't know how long it would have taken me to come to my senses."

"He is a good man, father. I hope he can forgive me for my strange actions and for leaving him without any consideration."

"I know he will, Annie. He is very fond of you. I believe he is still working at the mine in Timor. Although I am not sure how much longer he will find that profitable. He will probably find he needs to return to his father's property in Heathcote soon."

Her father's words made Annie anxious. She hoped he would come to talk to her before he made any plans to leave the mine.

Early the next morning, Rosa and Annie went for a walk down to the river and strolled along for quite a distance. There was a lot to catch up on. It reminded Annie of the long walks she had taken with her sister, Cora, and how they had both shared so many secrets. Rosa reminded her of Cora and she felt like a young child again as they sat together making daisy chains. But now she was the big sister, and she needed to make sure that Rosa was happy.

"Annie, I am so pleased that you have finally come home," said Rosa.

"It is lovely to be home too," replied Annie, threading another daisy onto her chain. "But tell me, what have you been doing? Have you kept up your piano practice?"

"Well, yes, I have, but changing schools again has been hard and I have to help mother, of course."

As they chatted, Annie could see that her responsibility as the oldest child had not affected Rosa badly. She seemed to be the same cheerful girl that Annie had left behind.

"Now that I am home, we must practice our duets some more," Annie smiled at her sister.

It took Annie some time to settle back into the routine of country life. She had become used to being told what to do and when to do it whilst in the asylum. So it was a strange feeling to be able to please herself whether or not she brushed her hair. It pleased her to sit by her mirror each night and run her brush through her tangled, unruly hair one hundred times in order to tame it somewhat.

She tried to spend as much time as possible out of doors. She was not entirely sure if the reason for this was really just her love of the garden or an attempt to spend less time with her stepmother.

She and her father had finally had a good long talk although it was quite a few weeks after she had returned before he opened up to her. He still seemed reticent to bring up anything that might upset her. He had shared with her the grief that he had felt at the loss of her mother. In return, she told him how she had found it so hard to see him so sad as she grew up and that she had tried everything she could to make him happy. It had seemed that nothing she did made any difference. She also told him how she felt left out and let down after having such a close and happy relationship with him. Now that they both had a better understanding of each other's feelings, they were spending more time together and had once again grown close. Annie was glad that the butcher shop had reopened and business, whilst not booming, was helping the family to survive. The situation was helped by the fact that Frederick was able to take on other carting and carpentry work as well.

Lillie had been kind to her since she had returned. Annie had felt the need to tell her how she had felt used and not a genuine part of the family. She told Lillie that she had felt like a slave. Now Lillie was not pushing her to help out, although Annie did still enjoy being with the children and helping them with their lessons and playing games with them. She kept her promise to Rosa, and they spent many hours together at the piano, playing duets. Gradually, the family joined them and it was almost like in the days when her mother was alive, when the family gathered around the piano and sang as Annie or Rosa played. Annie felt nostalgic at these times. Although they had a new family, she wondered if her father was also thinking back to the days when Ellen had been the one who played. At these times, he almost seemed his old self.

Despite the improved circumstances, Annie still felt rather confined in the family home. She had recently turned twenty and wanted a life of her own.

Chapter Twenty-Three

News travels fast in small towns, and soon neighbours and family friends were dropping into the Moore household to see Annie. Annie felt like a bit of a curiosity, but mostly people were kind and did not ask too many questions about her time in the asylum.

Eventually, the news must have made its way to the miners at Timor because Edmund paid a visit.

Annie was on her knees, pulling stubborn weeds from the garden. She was engrossed in her work and her knees and hands were covered in red earth. The sound of a horse trotting up the driveway caused her to look up. She could hardly believe her eyes. It was him. Edmund had finally come to see her.

"Annie," he called as he jumped down from his horse and flung the reins over the fence post.

Annie got to her feet, trying to brush off the dirt and tuck her hair back up under her bonnet. She felt her cheeks blush as she looked at him shyly, not sure how she should react or if indeed he would still have an interest in being reacquainted with her.

"Edmund, is it really you? I am so glad to see you. But I must look an awful mess."

Edmund laughed. "You are a sight for sore eyes, Annie. And how wonderful it is to see you too."

Edmund held out his hand, but Annie brushed it away.

"I need to wash up. Would you like a cup of tea?" Annie felt nervous at seeing Edmund after such a long time. Whilst she felt completely certain of her feelings for him, now seeing him in the flesh, she was not so sure that he would feel the same. He seemed so lively and handsome. Could she ever be enough for him?

"Yes, thank you. That would be lovely."

"Come inside and say hello to Mother and the children."

Annie led Edmund into the kitchen, where a fragrant odour of onions and mutton was emanating from the pot that Lillie was stirring. The boys were playing with a train set, the track winding around underneath the table. Their sister toddled around generally making a nuisance of herself, standing on the tracks. Rosa was helping her mother peeling vegetables for the stew, and the baby lay in her crib, gurgling happily to herself.

"Look who is here, Mother," said Annie. "Won't you sit down Edmund? I will wash up and then I can make you some tea."

As Annie left the room, Lillie greeted Edmund with a smile.

"Hello Edmund. It is lovely to see you. Yes, please do make yourself comfortable. The kettle is boiling, and I believe we have some fruitcake."

"Hello Mrs Moore," said Edmund politely. "It is quite a ride from Timor, so I would be very glad of a cup of tea."

"I am so glad you have come," said Lillie. "Annie has taken a while to settle back in, but I think she is getting along quite nicely now. She will be glad to renew your acquaintance, I am sure."

Annie came back into the room looking much improved after removing some of the dirt and releasing her hair from the bonnet and returning it to its fastenings. She moved around the kitchen, making tea and cutting large chunks of fruit cake.

"Why don't you take Edmund through to the sitting room?" said Lillie as soon as Annie had poured the tea.

Annie's hands shook as she placed the plate of fruit cake and the two cups of tea on a tray. She led Edmund through into the sitting room. Now there was nothing left to occupy her, so she sat down opposite Edmund and looked at him nervously.

"It really is good to see you, Edmund. How are you?"

"I am well and have been working hard. But how are you, Annie?" He looked at her anxiously.

"I am fine, thank you. It has been a very difficult time, but now that I have been home for a while, I feel a lot better. Mother has been kind and Father and I have spoken and resolved a few things." Annie looked down at her hands. She desperately wanted to apologise for the way she had left him, but the words simply would not come.

"How are things going at the mine?" she asked instead. "Father says that the gold could be running out."

"It is still working for the moment. But I think they will need fewer men as time goes on. The gold can't last forever. The shaft has gone very deep, down about 300 feet by now, and we bring up less and less each day."

"What will you do once the gold is gone?" asked Annie.

"I will have to go home to the farm in Heathcote. My father is not getting any younger and he will need my help. My brother wants to move to Melbourne. But let's not talk about all that now. How are you really, Annie? I have been so worried about you."

"I really am much better, Edmund. We have so much to talk about. But I would rather not talk about my absence. It is rather painful, and I just want to forget what happened."

"Very well, Annie," said Edmund, looking relieved that she didn't want to go into details. "There is a dance on Saturday night. Would you allow me to escort you?"

"That sounds delightful."

Edmund seemed pleased that she had accepted, so her spirits were buoyed.

Annie had grown stronger and more confident with each passing month. She and Edmund had become close again. Now almost a full year had passed since she had been released from the asylum.

It was a cold grey August day. Annie was longing for the summer. But it wouldn't be long now. The wattle trees were blossoming all around, holding the promise of spring.

Annie turned at the sound of a bicycle bell. The postman had arrived. She waved to the young man as he pulled his bicycle up at the front gate. It was always a treat to receive some mail.

"Hello Miss Annie. Mail for you today," he said as he handed her several letters.

"Thank you," she replied as she thumbed through the letters until she came to an envelope addressed to her. She thought she recognized the writing from the earlier letter she had received from Helena. She felt a gnawing guilt. She had not written to Helena with the news that she had been released. It had been many months since she had heard from her friend and she was a little afraid of what the letter might hold. What if she had not been able to cope with being back in the outside world? She took the precious letter to the verandah and sat down to read.

20th August 1895

My dearest friend Annie,

I wrote to you at the asylum, and Matron Lansdowne replied saying that you had been released. Oh, how my heart sang. That was just the most wonderful news. I hope you have settled back in at home. How is Edmund? Have you reconciled with him? I can imagine how happy that would make you. Please write back and tell me it is so.

But I also have news. Last month I gave birth to a beautiful baby girl. She is the light of my life. I cannot believe that the lord has granted me this blessing after all this time.

My husband has been wonderful, and he is also delighted with our beautiful daughter. He dotes on her.

Oh, but I have forgotten the most important news. We decided to call the baby Annie. What do you think? I hope you are pleased. I hope she grows up to be as beautiful and strong as you.

She is waking up now and will need to be fed, so I must go.

Please write soon to let me know how you are coping with being "outside" again. I know it took me quite a while to become reaccustomed to the freedom. But I am so happy, I can't tell you.

Your friend forever,

Helena

Annie was delighted to receive this news and was exceedingly happy for her friend. After all this time, Helena finally had the precious baby she had yearned for. Annie was truly honoured to have a new baby girl named after her. If only she could now have her own family and a baby of her own.

Chapter
Twenty-Four

The time of Edmund's departure was drawing near. The closure of the Grand Duke mine was only a few short months away. Although Annie was sad that Edmund would be leaving soon, she was pleased that he would not be working at the mine. It was becoming more and more dangerous as the shafts went ever deeper.

A few months ago there been a dreadful accident at the mine. Annie had been out shopping when she heard the news. She had purchased groceries for the family at the General Store and was just about to head to her father's butchery when a young woman entered the store.

"Have you heard the news?" she said to the shop assistant.

"No, what news?"

"There has been an accident at the Grand Duke mine. A miner has been killed. Apparently, there was a cave in and he was buried for nearly an hour. They said they could hear him moaning just before they finally got to him. But it seems it was too late. By the time the doctor arrived, he was pronounced dead."

"Oh, that is shocking," said the shop assistant. Then she noticed Annie still standing by the door. Her face had drained of all colour. "Are you alright Annie?"

Annie was stunned. She felt as if she might faint. What if it was Edmund? Eventually, she found her voice.

"Do you know who it was?" she asked.

"Oh Annie, I am sorry," said the shop assistant. "I forgot your beau works there. I am sure it won't be him."

"How can you be so sure?" Annie said as she turned to the bearer of the awful news. "So, do you know who it was?"

"I did hear a name, but I cannot be certain."

"Please, you must tell me. What is the name you heard?"

"I think it was John Casey."

Relief flooded through Annie as she realised it was not her Edmund. She immediately felt ashamed that she had not felt sympathy for the man concerned, but she could not help but be relieved. However, she would still worry until she saw Edmund in one piece again. She said a silent prayer for his safety but added a prayer for the poor young man and his family. She hurried to her father's butchery to tell him the news and then went home to wait to hear from Edmund. That evening he had ridden with all haste to see her to reassure her he was alright. She had never been so glad to see him.

"Oh Edmund, thank goodness you are alright," she said. "I was so worried. That poor man."

Edmund pulled Annie into a tight hug but immediately pulled back. Annie blushed. They were not even engaged yet.

"Yes, I am fine Annie. But everyone at the mine is shocked. It is the first time anyone has been killed at Grand Duke."

"Who was the young man?"

"His name was John Casey. He has a sister but she is his only family."

Annie was glad that Edmund had not been involved in the awful disaster but she could only imagine the terrible grief the victim's poor sister must be feeling. Knowing that she had no other family was shocking and Annie prayed that the woman would find support.

The day that Edmund proposed, for the second time, was vivid in Annie's memory. Edmund had been patient with her as she came to terms with her life after the asylum. He had waited over a year, but he would be leaving soon so could wait no longer. It was almost the same scene all over again, without the thunder storm and with a much different result. They had been to a town picnic and Edmund had walked Annie home. It was a beautiful calm summer evening. They sat on the front verandah of Annie's home watching the sunset. The sky glowed red, blue and gold, the colours changing every few minutes as the sun sunk slowly below the horizon.

"Annie, I will soon have to leave. And I know you have needed time to settle back into ordinary life. But you know of my regard for you," he said. He seemed too nervous to look at her as he said these words. Summoning up all his courage, he continued. He reached into the inside pocket of his jacket and once again produced the ring that he had held onto for all this time.

"Annie, I will need time to establish myself back on the farm, but eventually I want you to join me. Will you do me the honour of becoming my wife?"

This time Annie was firmly of one mind. She had no doubts.

"Yes, Edmund." It was all she could say. A huge smile lit up her face, and Edmund smiled in return. For Annie, it had been her dream for so long to become a wife and mother. Now she would have that chance.

Edmund pulled her to her feet, swept her up in a hug and whirled her around. Then he gently deposited the laughing Annie back on the ground and became serious again.

"Annie, you have made me so happy. I can't tell you." He kissed her gently, and they both knew that finally they would be together and everything would turn out well.

Annie sat on her bed daydreaming. It was four years since she had been released from the asylum and now it seemed a distant memory, though it sometimes still haunted her. All of her favorite things surrounded her. As the oldest sibling still living at home, she had a bedroom to herself. Her dresser was adorned with a photo of her family and a small one of Edmund. There were pots of cosmetics, and her ornate brush, comb and mirror set. But today her eye was drawn to her wedding gown, which hung resplendently on the wardrobe door, waiting for the big day.

Annie could not believe her dream was finally going to come true. In just a few short days she would marry Edmund and go to live with him on his family farm in Heathcote. Her whole body tingled as she thought of the moment when she would feel his arms around her again. She was nervous of course. It would be another big upheaval in her life.

She and Edmund had spent a lot of time together after Annie came home, whilst Edmund continued to work at the mine. Although Annie's family had moved back to Avoca, Edmund came to see her every weekend and they attended dances or the picnic races or simply spent time strolling along the banks of the Avoca river, quietly discussing the future.

The Grand Duke mine had closed down two years ago in 1896, so Edmund had moved back to his home to work on the family sheep farm. It had been a long engagement. He wanted time to establish himself and make a comfortable home for her before they married. Unfortunately, he had had some financial setbacks due to the continuing depression so more time had gone by than either of them would have liked. She missed him dreadfully of course and had longed for the time when they could finally be married. But she wrote to him at least once a week. Thankfully, he found time to reply nearly as often, so she was able to understand a bit more about his life and to keep their long distance love affair alive.

A knock on her bedroom door brought her abruptly back to the present. Rosa bounded into the room without waiting for permission from Annie to enter. Annie smiled at the exuberant young girl. She was still Annie's favourite of her half siblings. There were six of them now. Lillie had borne two more daughters since Annie had arrived back home.

Rosa had blossomed into a vibrant and pretty teenager with strong opinions, and she was not afraid to voice them. After all, whilst Annie had been away, she had taken on a bigger role of helping in the house and looking after the younger children. But she was not petulant, as Annie remembered she herself had been at the same age. She seemed carefree and happy, and Annie sometimes still felt slightly jealous of her. Annie knew Rosa would never be trapped and feel like a slave as she had when she was the same age. Rosa was there for her mother, but their relationship was so different. Although Lillie had her hands full with all the children, she seemed to have learnt that she needed to have a more compassionate approach. She had softened with the years. And in fact, Lillie and her father seemed very contented with their life.

Today, Annie was glad to have Rosa's company. The wedding day was approaching and all the plans were in place. Annie and her family would travel to Melbourne, where she was to be married in St Francis Catholic Church. She had kept up her religion in the asylum and when she had come home, so she was pleased to be married in a catholic church. She knew her mother would also be pleased and despite her happiness, she wished that her mother and Cora could be with her for her big day. Her faith was now a comfort to her once again. She was no longer intimidated by the hellfire and brimstone of her religion. She knew her mind, and she knew she wanted nothing more than to marry Edmund.

"Oh Annie, I do love your dress," said Rosa. Annie looked again, for the thousandth time, at the stylish white wedding dress. In some ways, it was quite plain, in that it lacked a lot of the lacy decorations that were currently fashionable. It was made from textured satin with the high-necked bodice gathered into the tiny waistband. Small pieces of delicate lace trimmed the neckline and peeked out at the cuffs of the full length sleeves. Annie did not plan to wear any other adornments or jewelery. However, it was her head wear that would make a statement.

"Oh, and your hat has arrived," said Rosa, spotting the large hat box. "May I see it? Please."

"I suppose you can if you can keep a secret," said Annie, amused at Rosa's excitement. She opened the box and carefully took out the hat. Rosa gasped.

"It is so beautiful. I know you said it would be tall, but I didn't think it would be that tall."

The hat had a wide, flat brim trimmed with lace. But the bows and twists on top were at least 12 inches tall.

Annie carefully placed the hat on her head. It was spectacular and just the statement that Annie wished to make on her wedding day. She was a strong and confident woman now, who knew her own mind and what she wanted from the rest of her life. She could not wait to marry Edmund and start her new life as a farmer's wife and hopefully soon as a mother, on Edmund's property in Heathcote.

Epilogue

Elsie arrived home after a difficult few days at the asylum. She was still struggling to be heard above the persistent voices of the men who did not want to relinquish any of the power they held over the female staff. It was frustrating but Elsie was determined to keep fighting for the rights of her inmates as well as women's rights in general. As she opened the door with a sigh of relief, she noticed that a letter had been dropped through the mail slot in her door. She didn't receive many letters so was curious to see who it was from.

She tore open the envelope and pulled out a Christmas Card and a letter. The card depicted a bush scene flanked by waratahs and sturt peas with families boiling the billy and enjoying a picnic. She turned the card over and realised it was from Annie. Elsie unfolded the letter and began to read.

15th December 1898

Dear Matron Lansdowne

I hope you are well. I am writing to say thank you for everything you did for me. I am grateful that I am now well and happy. Edmund and I were married on 26th October in St. Francis Church

in Melbourne. It was such a happy day with all my family in
attendance. I am on much better terms with my family now and
was happy that Edmund and I could be married in a catholic
church. My confusion about my religion has now been resolved
and it is still very important to me.

If you had not been so kind and helpful I might never have had
the courage to get well and escape from the confines of the asylum.

Please write back. I would really like to know how you are and
the progress you are making for women's rights. Wishing you a
very happy Christmas.

Your grateful friend,

Annie

Elsie smiled as she finished reading the letter. So Annie had
married Edmund. That news brought a wave of joy to her. She
hoped that Annie would soon have the family she longed for
and that Edmund would allow her to be her own woman. It
was frustrating to have to work so hard for women's rights. Bills
for Women's Franchise had been tabled at least fifteen times in
Victoria since 1891 but every time the bill had been voted down.
The Adult Suffrage Act had been passed in South Australia late
in 1894 and a bill was soon to be tabled in Western Australia so
surely there was hope. Despite the frustration of trying to make
her way in a man's world, Elsie was more determined than ever
to keep striving for women's rights.

Acknowledgements

Writing this book would not have been possible without help from many quarters. Historical fiction requires a lot of research in order that setting and real events depicted in the book are accurate for the place and time. I am always grateful for the historians whose diligent work paves the way for the authenticity that I hope is apparent in my writing. Whilst I relied on many sources one of note was *The World of Dolly Stainer*, the true story of a woman who spent most of her life in the Kew Lunatic Asylum. *The Mad Women's Ball* by Victoria Mas is a work of fiction but also provided inspiration. Additionally I am forever indebted to the National Library of Australia and its remarkable digital repository, Trove, which freely grants access to a wealth of primary sources. Ancestry was another great source for my work.

I acknowledge the invaluable contribution of my editor, Cecile Shanahan. Her meticulous attention to detail and insightful suggestions have shaped and enhanced the storyline. Without her expertise this book would not have reached its full potential. Thank you Cecile.

I hope you love the cover as much as I do. I was astounded when I first saw it. It was not what I imagined but so much more. I think it is simply stunning. Huge thank you to my book cover designer, Douglas Thomson from High Voltage Studio.

I am also very grateful for the support of several author groups. Write with Allison Tait, Writers Victoria Write Live, Jodi Gibson's Write Squad and The Curious Descendants Club. Members of all these groups have provided an indispensable source of inspiration to me.

To my early readers, Hannah Thomson and Heather Kelly, who took the time to read and provide feedback, thank you.

Finally, I would like to thank you, my readers. All those who read my debut novel, Conflict at Hanging Rock and all of you who I hope have enjoyed this book. Writing is a solitary pursuit for the most part, but to know that my work will be read encourages me to persevere.

Authors Note

I have been researching my family history for many years and I find it a rich source of ideas for my stories. This book is a work of fiction but is inspired by my Great Grandmother who spent eight months in the Kew Lunatic Asylum in 1894. I came across this startling fact whilst researching my family history on Ancestry and wondered how this had come about. The report stated that she had been brought to the asylum by police, suffering mania caused by religious excitement. The notes were very brief with only three additional entries. Apparently she had become more unsettled and violent and had to be confined to the refractory ward and later was "dull and stupid". Her discharge was noted briefly with the date.

As with my first novel, although many of the characters in this book are inspired by my ancestors, the names have been changed. I have done this in order to tell a complete story, as it may have happened, but much of it based on my imagination.

The terminology in this book is based on that used at the time when there was less understanding and empathy about mental illness. So in some cases it will seem offensive but in order to maintain the authenticity of the period I felt it was necessary to include these terms.

About the Author

Pauline Wilson lives in Yarrawonga in North East Victoria on the banks of the Murray River. She is a writer and family historian who loves learning and research. She writes historical fiction inspired by the lives of her ancestors. When she is not writing she likes to read, research her ancestors and take long walks by the river. Breaking Free is her second novel.

Connect on Instagram (@paulinemareewilson) or Facebook (@paulinewilsonauthor) or sign up for the latest news at www.paulinewilson.com.au/news

REVIEWS

Did you enjoy this book? You can make a big difference.

Honest reviews are the most powerful tools for getting my book noticed. So if you enjoyed this book I would I be very grateful if you could spend just a couple of minutes leaving a short review where ever you purchased this book.

Also By

Pauline Wilson

Conflict at Hanging Rock

Robert Blayney thought his live was over. But a twist of fate has landed him in Port Phillip clutching his ticket of leave.
Now he is left to his own devices to make his way into the interior in the early days of European settlement.
Soon the rest of his family join him, with the exception of his brother who is serving time in Van Diemen's Land.
As he becomes wealthy and his reputation as a gentleman grows, his desire to hide the secret of his convict past is thwarted by family conflict. When the family fued comes to a climax, will Robert lose all hope?
Meanwhile the growing community is struggling with a conflict of its own. Will the ongoing dispute over the use of the Hanging Rock Water and Recreation reserve ever be solved?